COMING HOME ON A KNOWN ROAD: A SUDANESE REFUGEE'S JOURNEY FROM WAR TO PROGRESS

Maker M. Marial

Acknowledgments

First, I would like to thank almighty God for his protection throughout my journey and every single day of my life. I also thank Patrick Hill for being inspirational behind the creation of this book. Patrick was inspired by my story when we first met in Nairobi, Kenya, in 2012, upon arrival from South Sudan, where he had visited Hope and Resurrection Secondary School with the mission team. After listening to my story, Patrick encouraged me to write a book. After my return from South Sudan in 2005, I had already drafted some chapters, but his encouragement motivated me more. I subsequently added more chapters and shared the first draft with him. He looked at it, did some editing and suggested more writing. This motivated me, and I continued writing. His encouragement kept me going despite many challenges. He told me that everything had "its perfect opportunity" and that I should continue. I also appreciate his suggestion that I reach out to Amazon for publication.

I also thank Patty Nicolas, my co-worker from the Senate Clerk's Office in the Commonwealth of Virginia. Her proofreading made the book flow well and interesting. I am thankful to Mary Higbee for her support in the initial stage of this project. Her feedback was rousing. I am also grateful to Tracy Kennedy, who spent time reviewing, editing and filtering the book to perfection. Tracy travelled with me to South Sudan in 2005 and was instrumental in shaping the book, particularly in the stories related to our trip. I am also thankful to Lisa Thompson for her great work of polishing the book by removing unnecessary things and suggesting the addition of new chapters to the book. She rearranged the book, and her final edits prepared it for the next step in its journey to publication.

I am also thankful to the Amazon Market Hub team for their great work. I am grateful to the Snr. Project Manager Harris Johnson for making sure that plans for the publication of this book went smoothly and timely. I am thankful to the cover designers and editorial team for doing a perfect job. I am also grateful to Jordon Lynch for responding to my online inquiries about the publication of this book and connection to the Amazon Marketing Hub's team.

I cannot find sufficient words to express my gratitude to my friends whose contribution of ideas and backing made the writing of this book possible. These special people include Majak M. Nyariel (Adomic), Peter M. Majang, Sunday J. Mabeny, Maker J. Mabok, Kuol A. Jok, Dut A. Yai, Garang K. Yai, Abraham D. Bul, Elijah A. Anyieth, Bol Bul, Peter Wal, and Athian Majak Akuemchol for his help with translation of some Dinka words to English.

Writing this book could not have been possible without the support of my family. Akot and Juma, thank you so much for your encouragement and support. I am also grateful to my mom and dad for making me who I am today. Their upbringing taught me to be courageous and a hard worker.

To my children, Toto, Eapen, Mabor, Yar and Aluet, thank you for your support and understanding. This project took away your valuable time, and I could not talk to you on the phone as it used to be or spend time with you whenever I had an opportunity to come home from work.

To my lovely wife, Angelina, thank you so much for being a caring and supportive woman. Your encouragement kept me going even when I struggled to put my thoughts together and almost gave up. I am grateful to you for taking good care of our kids and home while I was away for humanitarian work in a remote part of the country.

My deepest appreciation goes to Patricia Satterfield (RIP) for her care and support. I also thank her husband, Jim, for making me part of their family. I am also grateful to Sari and George Eapen for their love and support. It wouldn't have been possible for me to complete my education in the U.S. without their kindness. I also thank them for their continued care. I am also thankful to Jennifer and Darryl Ernst for making me part of them. I also thank them for everything they do to help me.

I am grateful to Susan C. Schaar for the opportunity to work in the Senate Clerk's Office in the Commonwealth of Virginia. The four years I spent there sharpened my political thoughts. I also thank John Garrett for being a great monitor and appreciate all the Senate Clerk's Office staff for their love and support. With their kindness, I was able to adapt to the system and learn how to do things perfectly.

Finally, to my Political Science Professor, Nelson Wikstrom, thank you so much for empowering my political thoughts. I appreciate your friendship, support and connection, which led me to finding a job in the Senate Clerk's Office.

Disclaimer

The content of this book is based on true stories and real-life events, however, it should be noted that some elements of fiction have been added for creative purposes. The information presented in this book may not be completely accurate or reflect real-life events exactly as they occurred. This book is intended for spreading awareness only and should not be relied upon for factual information. The author makes no representations or warranties with respect to the accuracy or completeness of the contents of this book. The reader is encouraged to use their discretion when interpreting the events described in this book.

In memory of Patricia G. Satterfield.

Table of Contents

Introduction

As Sudan's civil war deepened in the mid-1980s, and the villages in southern Sudan were being attacked and destroyed one after the other, children as young as five years old were being separated from their families and forced to walk thousands of miles in the hope of finding protection in refugee camps.

Many young people struggled to survive alone in the refugee camps without families or guidance and not knowing what had happened to their relatives during attacks on their villages. Some died of hunger and treatable diseases. Others developed mental problems as a result of untreated depression.

Despite these challenges, many of these boys and girls overcame the encounters and excelled in life. Those who were fortunate enough to be adopted by western countries could begin new lives and get an education. Many returned home to reunite with their families and take part in rebuilding their homeland, which emerged from the war as the independent nation of South Sudan.

My book is a story of my life as one of many Sudanese children who experienced the effects of the civil war. Separated from my family and ended up in alien lands, I struggled with life for years before being selected to be part of the resettlement program that sent thousands of young Sudanese (who later became known as the Lost Boys and Girls of Sudan) to the United States of America. There, I was able to fulfil my dream of better education and return home years later for a reunion with my family.

I hope the rendering of my life's journey inspires you, as it has me, to carry on in the face of adversity and never lose hope.

Forward

My friend, Maker Marial, grew up navigating a life of constant, catastrophic change. He discovers early on that his bucolic childhood is interrupted at a very young age by a horrific, never-ending civil war that claims the lives of more than two million South Sudanese and sends Maker on a survival trajectory that rivals no other. Yet, in the terror of it all, Maker perseveres and valiantly honours his namesake: Maker.

Maker, in the Dinka language of South Sudan, translates as "white and black bull". While that typifies a cow, in Maker's world, that white and black bull signifies power and providence. Farming and keeping livestock is the livelihood of the people of Karic in the Lake States, Maker's home. Yet, when Maker witnesses his neighbours and friends shot to death, and their tukuls set aflame, he becomes more than a simple farmer. With bullish persistence and trust in an almighty God, Maker spends his formative years fervently escaping the brutal enemy. He journeys for weeks and months fending off the attacks, not just from Arab troops from the north, but from wild animals, deadly diseases, and starvation while searching for his family. Months lead to years in refugee camps. Twenty years will pass before Maker once again reunites with his father. Maker Marial is most certainly a bull of a man.

Early on, Maker comes to value the importance of education as a means to justice. As he purposefully pursues his education, Maker finds his studies repeatedly interrupted due to civil unrest throughout the region and even in the refugee camps. But he does not give up. After years in the camps and hope dwindling for any return home, Maker is approached by the resettlement program, the Lost Boys and Girls of Sudan. Through the Lost Boys and Girls, Maker can continue with his dream. Several false starts eventually land Maker in Richmond, Virginia. Maker is a quick study. In striving for his GED, his English dramatically improves, and he enrols in college. He takes on a part-time job. His trust in God never wavers. Through his most loving and devoted sponsors, Darryl and Jennifer Ernst, I met Maker while serving as assistant rector with Christ Church, Glen Allen, just west of Richmond. With the never-failing support of many, especially the Ernsts, the church, and the ever-growing South Sudanese community now established in Richmond, Maker excels. He graduated from Virginia Commonwealth University with a Bachelor of Arts degree in Political Science and a minor in Criminal Justice. He then goes on to achieve a master's degree in Public Administration from VCU.

His passion for education as the pathway to achieving truth and justice continues. Maker is instrumental in helping the young people of South Sudan, deprived of education and opportunity, to find a future. Along with the Ernsts, Christ Church, and others, Maker helps pave the way for the establishment of Hope and Resurrection Secondary School in Atiaba, not far from his hometown of Karic.

Rather than a battle for liberation through combat and war, Maker learns through his arduous journey that education is the resolution to the conflict. He returns to South Sudan to serve as a model of hope and possibility for those so crippled by the effects of the war. He marries his love, Angelina, and together they raise their family. Grateful for the wisdom he has gained through his life experience, and especially his pursuit of education, Maker finds himself employed in humanitarian work. Since his return to his homeland more than seven years ago, Maker has served with several NGOs in different positions and currently as a field area coordinator with Catholic Relief Services (CRS).

<u>Coming Home on a Known Road</u> is the story of one man's remarkable journey through what appears to be a course of hopelessness. Maker Marial, instead, chose to live up to his name. Bullish throughout, but with kindness, love, and a genuine desire to make his world, and the world of his people, a better place, Maker

soldiers on to show us all God's light of hope shining fervently through the trees.

—The Rev. Hillary, West Charlottesville, Virginia

My Search for Security and Family

It was always under the moonlight and bright stars when the children of Karic would go out to play. Karic is a village located east of Rumbek, the present capital of Lakes State. In this village, there was no electricity or running water, no tarmac road, hospital, or well-supplied schools and markets. The livelihood of about 200 families depended largely on their small-scale farming and livestock rearing. They used traditional medicines to treat diseases when they got sick. Moonlight was the electricity for the people of Karic, allowing them to practice their traditional dances free from the usually sweltering heat and daytime chores such as cultivation, harvesting, and herding of livestock.

The people of Karic had never experienced the amenities of large cities. Just a few of the villagers had a chance to visit nearby Rumbek, 30 miles to the west. Rumbek was made up of a few modern buildings with hundreds of tukuls (traditional thatched roof houses). It had a dirt main street and a dirt airstrip. There were no tall buildings, no malls or communication towers. There was only the Rumbek Hospital which always lacked medicines. Many patients admitted to the hospital lacked beds and usually used traditional mats to sleep under trees on the hospital grounds.

Just a few miles south of Rumbek, there was a huge military presence at the Malou Military Barracks. There was also a huge police force deployed in town for unknown reasons at that time. They left behind the comforts of north Sudan, which I heard had all the beautiful things we didn't have in the south, such as paved roads, good schools, markets, hospitals, tall buildings, and electric lights.

These armies were deployed by the Arab-dominated government in Khartoum to protect their interests or fight the rebels in the south. The war had been going on in the region for four years. Rumours of villages being attacked and lives shattered by Arab troops from the north were heard by the people of Karic, but few thought it would reach their village.

However, it was just after this carefree and joyful night that the Sudanese civil war finally reached the village and affected our lives. I had joined the children in the village that night in Diany (girls' traditional dance); and Alueeth (boys' play).

When these animated games and dances ended, and everybody dispersed, I went with my cousins to their house and spent the night with them. In Dinka culture, young boys and girls spend their early years together. Young males eat from house to house and sleep in one of the houses they have chosen, and the females do the same. This part of our culture allows the youths to grow and learn the values of hard work, respect and responsibility from each other. Always being together allowed youths, particularly the males, to bond and learn from each other and become future warriors who can defend their clan or tribe against internal and external foes. I was nine years old and loved the close kinship of cousins and friends. I felt lonely when I was not with them.

We grew tired of our games in the moonlit hours, so we went home and straight to bed. It was a beautiful night with cool weather. We fell asleep immediately like babies, with no time even for the bedtime stories we usually told in turn. The cool morning breeze and the sounds of birds singing and cock crowing made our rest even more pleasant. Our plan was to sleep in because we usually took our goats for grazing in the afternoon. Our local Karic Primary School was closed for a two-week break, so we had lots of time to enjoy some idle pursuits with the other children in the village.

As we lay motionless on our sleeping mats, a loud explosion rocked the village. Everybody in the room was awakened and tried to understand what was happening. More bombs were falling, and their terror was reinforced by all kinds of gunfire. There was a commotion as everybody in the village tried to escape the attack. We raced outside, running in all directions. Everybody was confused as people tried to run or take cover. The troops, dressed in green uniforms and heavily armed with lethal weapons, had secretly surrounded the village overnight before they launched their early morning attack. Within a few minutes of the raid, the whole village was already on fire and engulfed in smoke. Many people in the neighbourhood, along with goats and sheep, were shot dead or burned alive in their tukuls. Some people, mostly women and children who were spared the enemy's bullets, were dragged away and thrown in military trucks to be taken away after the raid. Most animals from the village were killed; nothing was left breathing in the village after the attack.

As everybody ran in different directions for safety, it was hard to catch up with my cousins or my parents. I ran by myself while praying to God that no bullet should strike my tiny body. I was crying and calling for my parents with no response. I was deafened by the sound of the guns and explosions. Although the morning air was still cool, my body was already wet with sweat.

As I took off from the house, my uncle, Majak, saw me running and was trying to get a hold of me, but I was sprinting as fast as I could and couldn't hear him. Trying to save me from falling into the enemy's hands, my uncle finally caught up to me and grabbed my hand. We ran to nearby woods together and hid there while the killings in the village raged on. My heart almost stopped when he grabbed my hand. I thought the enemy had caught me and that my life would be over. However, when I turned my head and saw my uncle holding my hand, I was happy and relieved. I asked him if he had seen my parents, three brothers, my sister, my cousins, and his children, but he said he had not.

It was a great stroke of luck that my uncle's house was located near the bushy area. No one could see us once we were in there. Those woods became our home for the next three days. The village went quiet just hours after the attack. The wounded who did not immediately succumb to their wounds were now dead after many hours on the ground. There was no life in the village. The only living things were vultures and other scavengers that were feasting on the bodies. We could see and smell the houses burning from our hideout, but we were afraid to go and inspect the area.

After three days, hungry, cold, and worried about the rest of our families, my uncle told me that he wanted to go to the village and see whether survivors had returned to the devastated village. I thought that it was still too dangerous for him to go there, but he insisted he should go, and he went. After a time in the village, my uncle returned and told me that he couldn't find any members of our families or their bodies in the village. He added that most villagers were dead, and nothing was left there.

"Most of the village's livestock is dead. The grain storage huts were looted, and whatever was left was set ablaze. Now we must move away from here for our safety," he said.

"Where are we going, uncle?" I asked.

"Where we will find our families and be safe," he replied.

I agreed, and we started walking, heading east of Karic. We had a small container of water and a few peanuts in a tiny bag he brought with him after he went to the village. The few clothes we had on our bodies were the only things we brought to wear. We didn't have shoes as we lost them during the attack. Walking barefoot became my biggest challenge. Thorns and other sharp objects were hurting my feet, and within a few days, I could barely walk. My feet had developed painful blisters as our journey intensified.

We decided to walk at night when it was cold and hide in the bushes during the day. Our hope was to find our families and safety. Feeding only on peanuts and water for two days had already given me a stomachache and began to weaken me, but I told myself that I must be brave enough to keep on walking.

After an overnight journey, we arrived at a town called Yirol. Yirol was part of Lakes State and under the control of the Sudan People's Liberation Army (SPLA). The rebels had liberated this town and had been controlling it for three years. This town wasn't a safe place for Internal Displaced Persons (IDPs) either; the northern warplanes bombed it day and night in attempts to flush out the rebels.

Soon after our arrival, we were told that we should dig ourselves a trench in which we would take cover during the frequent air raids. We were told by many IDPs who had been there that air attacks were constant, and many died as a result. After hearing this news, my uncle decided that we shouldn't stay in this town long and that we should start going somewhere that would be safe for us. "The bombs from Northern Sudanese aeroplanes will kill us if we stay here," he said.

During our overnight walk to Yirol, we came upon village after village that was destroyed, and many of their inhabitants were slaughtered by the Arab troops. We were scared as we didn't come upon anyone along the way to tell us the direction we should take to avoid falling into the hands of the northern armies.

In Yirol, however, we met many families who were fleeing their villages after attacks like we had in Karic. Everyone was missing at least a family member. Many children of my age or younger were wandering by themselves with no parents to look after them.

Four days had passed since our last meal, so we hoped to find something to eat in town. As we set out to find food, we noticed that many people were transfixed by an unusual sound. They seemed to freeze and grow quiet. Before we could understand what was happening, the first explosion sounded a few feet from us, followed by several more. Within the next few minutes, countless more of these bombs landed. The area was clouded with dust and smoke, the injured were groaning, and we saw many of the innocents lying dead. They were cut into pieces, and some were missing their hands or feet. Over the next hours, more planes were pounding the town. The assault went on until nightfall.

Everybody was grabbing their belongings and heading east of the town. We took what we had and followed them. It was a chaotic scene as everybody was trying to get away from the terror. In this process, the unaccompanied children who were as young as 5 or 6 years old were crying as they didn't know what to do. Some just followed the crowds, while others just sat and cried. Some older people were compassionate towards these kids and carried them.

I didn't know where we were going, but my hope was that I would find my family. We met a huge crowd in Yirol, and this made me optimistic that there was a possibility of finding my family among the IDPs. I was very hungry and tired from our walk the previous night.

After the overnight walk, we arrived at a place called Shambe on the western bank of the River Nile. This is the port where the SPLA used barges and carved-out canoes to ferry their military equipment and soldiers to the other side. It was the first time I ever saw such a big river. I had been to Lake Akeu, Lake Nyibor and Bahr El Naam which were all located in the Rumbek region, but nothing among them looked like the River Nile.

We were exhausted and reclined under trees to sleep. There were some IDPs who were waiting to be helped across the river. I didn't bother to go and look among the crowds for my family as I was very tired, hungry, and sleepy. There was nothing to eat except for the peanuts we had carried from home. Some fishermen had caught a lot of fish, but I had no interest in approaching and begging them for fish. My uncle had already fallen asleep, and I was ready to follow suit. Now I was feeling drowsy and went and laid next to him and slept.

In the afternoon and after several hours of good sleep, we awoke to the delicious smell of cooked fish. The SPLA soldiers who welcomed us at this port had collected a good number of fish from the fishermen and cooked them in big pots to feed the hungry crowds. My feet were blistered and in excruciating pain. I was also very weak because I didn't have enough to eat during the previous five days. There were ten lines leading up to each pot which were full of cooked fish. One of the soldiers directed the two of us to one of the pots, where we waited for our turn to be served. We received the tasty fish. The flavour of the fish was enhanced by the fact that we had not eaten for so long.

It was now late in the afternoon, and the SPLA soldiers began loading into barges and boats the groups of IDPs who were there before us and ferrying them to the other side of the River Nile. I was told by my uncle that they were being taken to a safe place on the other side of the river. But he wasn't sure where exactly. The SPLA soldiers were stationed here to help their fellow soldiers cross to either side of the river with their weapons and ammunition. They also had a mission to guard the port against invasion by the northern troops and to help civilians cross to the other side.

Seeing these people leave for the other side of the river made me very anxious to find out whether my family had been in the crowds. I didn't have a chance to look for them when we arrived at the port because I was exhausted. My hope was that I would have enough time to look for them after I recovered from the long-distance walk. With the first groups leaving, I thought it was not going to be possible again to meet up with these groups. So, I rushed to the port and saw everyone getting into the barges or boats. After the last boat was loaded, my hopes of finding any members of my family were dashed. My journey was inspired, in large part, by the thought that I would find my family among the multitudes that gathered at this port, but now it seemed impossible. I lost this hope and went back to where we were sitting.

It was getting dark, and mosquitoes had already launched their attack on us. We didn't have mosquito nets, and they began to feast on us. We tried in vain to swat them away or crush them when we felt the bites on our bodies. We protected our mouths and noses as we were afraid that if bugs got in, we would suffocate and die. That whole night, we stayed awake fighting the Nile's mosquitoes.

Early in the morning, we heard the terrible news that one of the barges had capsized in the middle of the Nile, and all of its more than 200 passengers were feared dead. It was sad news for all of us, though none among them was our relative. Details emerged that passengers on board were ripped apart by crocodiles soon after they hit the water, and the water on the scene of the incident was covered with blood. I was sad and scared at the same time.

The barges and boats would take two days to come back and be loaded with more IDPs. I expected that the next trip would be our turn to cross to the other side of the river. I was afraid of a similar incident, particularly with the crocodiles in the river, but there was no other choice. We would not sleep day or night while waiting for the boats because of the mosquitoes. Many refugees were already infected with malaria and dying. I was afraid and didn't want to die before seeing my family. The soldiers here were very kind; they were feeding the IDPs and sharing with them the little malarial medicines they had, though many were too far gone and died.

After two days, the barges and boats docked at the port, and everybody was told to be ready to leave in the morning. We got ready and left on the first barge. It took us a few hours to arrive at the port outside Mading, a provisional town in the present Jonglei State. As we sailed along the Nile, we enjoyed its aquatic life and scenery. It was green with many kinds of animals that were the inhabitants of its beautiful islands.

After getting off these barges, we were about to be led to Baidit to join up with the IDPs who were brought ahead of us. Baidit village was the SPLA's base outside Mading, but its inhabitants were under constant air raids from the Khartoum regime, as the town of Yirol, which we left a few days ago. As we got close to the village, a voice said, "Everybody lie down, lie down." Everybody started to hit the ground, and there was a huge explosion which was followed by many more. There was huge smoke and the grass we were in caught on fire. As the smoke cleared, our line had been hit badly, and many innocent souls were already lying dead. My uncle Majak was one of them. Looking down at his lifeless body, I felt shocked, confused and abandoned! I continued to stand there whilst everybody else took cover to avoid being hit. I had lost my will to survive and wished the warplane would quickly return and hit me. It was the gloomiest moment of my life.

The plane came and dropped more bombs, and many more souls were taken, but I wasn't hit, which upset me more. Everybody was in survival mode and looking for a place that would be safe for them. I didn't want to leave. I imagined that I would die there, too. A lady named Ayen had been with us since we left Yirol, and she did not want to leave me there and insisted that I go with her and her two sons. She said there was nothing I could do since my uncle was dead and that it would be better for me to go with her. She grabbed my hand and pulled me away from the scene as I fixed my eyes on my uncle's torn body. Hastily, we disappeared from the scene, and for the next few days, I cried daily. I felt like it was the end of my world. I lost my family, my village, my friends, my cousins and now an uncle who had been taking care of me since the attack on Karic.

The air attacks did not stop. The village of Baidit was bombed throughout the night, and everybody was forced to leave the village heading east. We arrived in Anyidi after many hours of walking. This village was an assembly point for all the displaced persons heading to refugee camps in Ethiopia. From here, our journey for the next two and half months had just begun.

Soon after leaving the village of Anyidi, we stepped into the flood water, breaking and sleeping only in some of the few islands we found on our way. This would continue for about a month. Food was becoming rare, while mosquito attacks became more problematic than the bombs from the Sudanese Air Force.

Just five days into our walk, many people began losing their toes while others had their feet cut by objects in the water. Some of the injured got bad infections and remained in the water. The lucky ones with infected wounds managed to walk through the flood water with their badly swollen feet. Ayen tried to fulfil her promise that she would take good care of me and made sure that I had at least a spoonful of peanut butter daily and in her company. She had two sons, one my age and another who was a little older. They were both good boys and treated me like their brother.

After a few weeks, many died of malaria and other diseases, while some were killed by crocodiles. You could see someone in front of you falling and disappearing because of being grabbed by a gigantic crocodile, pulled underwater and torn to pieces while everyone watched helplessly.

At some points, the water level could reach as high as my neck, but I held my neck high until I reached the shallow waters. Walking in the water was very exhausting, and many could walk no further and were left there to die. I was motivated by one thing: finding my family. I didn't want to die before I found them. I was hoping that the place where people were heading would be where I would find them.

After walking in the flood waters for almost a month now, we reached a dry area where we would face more challenges than in the waters. We were tired and hungry and mourned those we lost along the way. Many argued that the groups should take time to relax and recover from the exhaustion, but others who perceived the unfolding dangers along our way insisted that we should always keep walking until we found a safe place. Sometimes, it would be agreed that we rest for a day or two in one of the abandoned villages and look for food there. In these villages, people would go through the tukuls and look for grains that would be boiled and eaten like that. Eating boiled grains became another problem for people who had gone for almost a month without enough to eat. Many developed stomachaches and diarrhoea. There were no medicines, and people would die. I was spared from the stomach problem. It may have been because Ayen fed me a spoonful of peanut butter every day. She was a kind woman and treated me like her own son.

In these villages, the debate would continue among the old folks about whether we rest longer in this place or leave. Some were afraid that if we stayed longer, the government-allied militias suspected of burning down this village would come and attack us if they found out we were there. During our walk, we came upon village after village that was destroyed and with dead bodies lying everywhere. This would put fear in many people and prompt us to leave immediately. I was one of the folks who always wanted to leave the area, not because of the fear of militia but because of the hope that my parents might be where we were going. So, I followed the crowd.

As darkness approached, we left the village, heading east. It was ordered that everyone must be in one line, and we would rest once the lead person decided it was necessary to take a break. We went through vast land with no trees but with short grass. Water was lacking as we went further. It was getting darker as clouds were building in the sky, and then some rain showers. No one in the group had a flashlight, and we couldn't see anything. We were told to grab and hold on to someone in front while we continued our journey.

The wild animals sensed us and followed us. We could hear lions and hyenas approaching from both sides. Everybody was scared by this, but there was nothing we could do. The animals started their attack on us simultaneously, and we could hear the cries of people as they were being torn into pieces and eaten alive. Throughout the night, many people were being snatched in front and behind as we walked. We couldn't stop because the animals would kill more people. We walked throughout the night, and the animals stopped only after they felt that they were well-fed.

After daybreak, we camped in an area with some trees. We counted our losses to the animals overnight and realized many didn't survive. After resting in this area with a little food and very little water, we set out for our journey in the evening and continued throughout the night, going through conditions like the night before. We arrived at Pibor, where we rested before taking off again in the evening. For the next two weeks, we experienced animal attacks and water and food shortages. Many people were killed by wild animals, while many others died of starvation and dehydration. Many gave up on this long journey and were left to die. It was an exhausting journey that cost many lives.

Our last journey was very tiresome, with no water or food. All of us were near death. We had been walking for three months now, but no one seemed to know where we were going. Even my hopes for finding my family were waning. I was tired. My feet were blistered. I was growing very weak daily and didn't want to continue with this painful journey anymore. I had told Ayen that I had given up on my life and I wouldn't continue with them, but she said that she didn't want me to die there.

"I want you to be reunited with your family, and that will happen only if you continue with us," she said.

One morning, as I was near death and worried that I wouldn't survive the day, I smelled the water of a river nearby, and my spirits soared. This meant food and water for us. Despite my weakness, I stood up and saw some structures like tukuls in the distance. I couldn't believe it. I rubbed my eyes and opened them again, and it was real. I was excited; however, I was afraid that the dwellings could be for the government-allied militias or a deserted village as we had often found along the way. I went back to Ayen and told her what I saw, and she stood up to see for herself. She burst into laughter and said, "We have survived," and everybody stood up and saw the tukuls. It was still early in the morning, and everybody was anxious to know what was in those structures. The whole group then moved closer to them, and we found out that the place was an assembly point for all the IDPs heading to various refugee camps in Ethiopia. Our three-month journey had brought us to Pochalla, a Sudan-Ethiopia border town. We stayed in Pochalla for one week to rest, then embarked on another difficult journey going through the terrain of mountains, hills, and valleys before crossing the River Raad to Dimma. In Dimma, we were received by the SPLA and Ethiopian Government representatives who ran the camp.

Dimma Refugee Camp

Established in January 1986 by the Administration of Refugee and Returnee Affairs (ARRA), an Ethiopian government's relief wing, the Dimma Refugee Camp held a population of several thousand refugees who were primarily Sudanese. On arrival, we were given food, clothing, sleeping materials and cooking utensils. Medical staff also came and checked us. Those with blisters on their feet and other medical issues were treated there. I was very tired but excited to have survived a three-month walk which covered about 1,600 miles, made worse by attacks from lions and hyenas, dehydration, and starvation. I was excited to see many people living in this place and was hoping that my family would be here, too. Our food was mainly maize grains, and with no flour or anything better. Hungry as we were, people started boiling the maize grains. Some didn't let it cook well before filling their stomachs which had been without adequate food for months. As a result, many had a stomachache and became sick.

After spending a day in this transit camp, our group was divided into two, one for unaccompanied minors such as myself and another for refugee families. Once again, I was separated from someone whom I had called mom since the death of my uncle. I was taken to a place where I didn't know anybody. I was worried and afraid that my life would be in greater danger since I was going to leave with people I didn't know. I sadly said goodbye to my surrogate mom, Ayen, and her two sons, Makuac and Deng, as we were separated against our wills.

I joined the group with children below the age of 14. I was nine years old, and many of the children were as young as five-years-old. We were escorted to the Dimma Refugee Camp, which was just a few meters from where we were. This camp had thousands and thousands of unaccompanied children under the responsibility of the Southern Sudanese. Hundreds of them shared a big hut they built themselves. There were hundreds of these huts everywhere in the camp, including some that served as classrooms. There were a few older folks here but not a single woman. They were the teachers, Southern Sudanese, who were deployed by the SPLA to teach the children affected by war how to read and write in English. The camp was run like a military barracks. Everything was done through someone else's orders, and no one was supposed to do anything without asking for permission from someone above.

Upon arrival, we found some young boys waiting for us. They were the leaders in charge of the huts. They had a few of their teachers with them. The policies and rules of the camp were quickly explained to us. We were told that everybody in the camp worked hard daily apart from going to classes. It was further explained that some of the work we would be doing included washing teachers' clothes, cooking, going to the forest to cut grass and poles for construction and pounding maize grains for one's own platoon. The schooling, we were told, would be done alternatively; some students would be going to their classes in the morning while others would be going in the evening after completing their tasks. Those taking their classes in the morning would cook for their respective groups in the evening, while those for evening classes would go to the forest in the morning to fetch construction materials and get back in the afternoon before their classes. It was explained that whoever failed to conform to the rules was punished severely. The boys fetched construction materials for building teachers' houses and those of the other leaders who were assigned to the camp.

After all of this, I became afraid and worried for my life. My hopes for finding my family now seemed to be just a dream. After long explanations of these policies, each leader among the boys was asked to take a few of us with him. I was taken and shown a bed in a big hut. This bed was made of tree poles and sticks on top, which were covered with old empty maize sacks. There were no bed sheets or mosquito nets. The tukul was big and housed about 200 boys. There were rows of beds in each aisle and a hallway in the middle. The leaders charged at people early in the morning when they were still sleeping. They would come into the room with sticks at around four in the morning and wake people up by beating them. People would assemble outside before being dispatched to the mountainous, thick forest to fetch construction materials. People left without eating breakfast and got back at around two or three in the afternoon. There wasn't any breakfast in the camp.

Each day many people would fail to come back because they were mauled by lions or got lost in the thick forest. After just two days of rest, I was introduced to these routines. At first, it was very difficult but after a week or so, I became used to it. The worst part of fetching these materials was that a group of ten people could share one blunt axe. There weren't any tools in the camp, so people could use only what they had at their disposal. Some used stone instead of waiting for hours for the same axe. This wasn't always an easy job. It was tough as people hurt their hands with the sharp stones.

I had been in this camp for more than a month, yet I was still very tired and recovering from the three-month walk. I was thinking about my family and uncle Majak. I couldn't sleep.

We headed to the forest, which took several hours. There were 15 of us in a team. We carried water in jerrycans, as we were told the water was essential to spending hours in the forest. There was no food or anything, just water. We would spend six to seven hours, depending on how much faster we could each cut down a tree. Five of us were new to the area and were scared as we approached the deep forest. Our fears were made worse when the group leader, who I believe was 10 years old, traumatized us with stories of boys who had strayed too far from the group. Several had died there, and their bodies could not be traced. We gladly followed his instructions to stay together.

As we entered the forest, we heard a voice from above saying, "help me, help me, help me!" We all rushed there and saw a young boy in a tree. He climbed a tree after his group was attacked, and six of the 20 boys were killed by lions the day before. He survived the attack because he outran the lions and climbed the tree. We could see many of the human remains scattered everywhere in the woods. We were scared and urged the boy to come down, and we quickly left the area for another area where we felt safe and were able to cut down trees.

After six hours in the deep forest, we headed back to the camp carrying our poles. We arrived after a two-hour walk, tired and hungry and dropped our poles on the ground. We assembled under a shade of a tree in the middle of the campus, and we were counted and told about our next job. Our next job would be to bury two boys, ages 8 and 10. They were critically ill when I arrived. I was told they were suffering from malaria and some other unknown diseases. We shared the same room. They were just skeletons after being sick for months without proper medical care. Now we were asked to go and bury them. Boys burying boys.

We took the bodies to a nearby graveyard and buried them in one shallow grave. The graveyard was full of graves. Many boys were dying daily of starvation, diarrhoea, and other diseases. I was scared, as I had just been introduced to burying people for the first time since I was born. What I knew from my village in southern Sudan was that children of my age or young people, in general, were not allowed to bury a dead person or even come near a burial site. It was a cultural belief. Because of this, I was worried about my life and thought I would be the next. After the burial, we came back to the camp and ate the little food that was waiting for us. The next day we went back again to the forest to fetch construction poles. This was our routine for the next four years while many boys were dying daily. Apart from hard labour, any mistake by one boy could lead to everyone being punished. Life was very difficult. I went to school in the evening but could hardly understand things.

I couldn't see Ayen with her two sons, though I believed their camp was not far from ours. We were not allowed to go to a nearby market or other nearby camps. If you were found there, you would be beaten. I didn't want to risk my life by seeing them and resigned myself to the camp instead. I thought about my family day and night. I hoped that they might be in one of the camps nearby.

For four years, I struggled with this. I couldn't understand what had happened to my family. There were no telephones or any other means of communication in the camp. We heard about the news in Sudan when new refugees arrived in our camp, but there was never news about my family. I prayed for the safety of my parents, brothers, and sister day and night.

Over time things were not going well in the camp. The relationship between the boys in the camp and the local Kachipo and Ngalam communities were deteriorating fast. Boys were sneaking into their farms and stealing their corn and other products. This led to the killing of some boys by Kachipo and Ngalam and brought a terrible clash between refugees and the Kachipo and Ngalam communities in 1988. Many lives were lost as a result. After this clash, the security in the camp became terrible. Boys were being killed daily everywhere, on the fishing grounds or in the forest where they fetched construction materials.

The bad relations continued for years and became worse in May 1991, when rebels, the Ethiopian Peoples' Revolutionary Democratic Front (EPRDF), overthrew the Mengistu regime. The EPRDF, headed by Meles Zenawi, and a host of other rebel coalition groups, including the Oromo Liberation Front (OLF) and the Tigrayan Peoples' Liberation Front (TPLF), later established a coalition government known as the Transitional Government of Ethiopia. This new government didn't want refugees in Ethiopia.

In 1974, Mengistu Haile Mariam led a rebellion that overthrew the monarchical rule of Emperor Haile Selassie, who had ruled Ethiopia for decades. Mengistu ruled for more than 17 years in a most repressive manner, perpetrating serious human rights abuses under a

Marxist-style government that did not tolerate dissent or opposition. This led to many factions in the country and a long civil war.

During the rebels' advance to overthrow the Mengistu regime, the refugees were not spared; they were being killed by the rebels and their coalition. The rebels suspected the SPLA, who then had training camps in Ethiopia, of supporting Mengistu against them. The SPLA was believed to have had backing from the Mengistu regime as it fought a war with Khartoum. This had terrible consequences for the innocent refugees who were in the Ethiopian land for safety.

As rebels advanced toward the camps after the fall of major cities across Ethiopia, refugees were asked to leave the camps and head back to southern Sudan. This created chaos as many refugees were afraid to go back to their homeland after escaping death on the journey to reach the camps. Some refugees picked up and headed back, while others were reluctant. I heeded the call and crossed the border back to southern Sudan the evening the announcement was made.

Two days later, Ethiopian rebels attacked the camp. Thousands of refugees tried to flee, and many of them drowned in the Raad River. The river was overflowing, and the currents were high. People have swept away as they jumped into the water to escape the bullets from the attackers. Thousands of refugees lost their lives in the river and at the hands of the rebels. It was sad to see innocent people die just like that.

The survivors then came to Pakok in Jonglei, a border town in southern Sudan. Some had gunshot wounds, but there was no medical care. There were no UN agencies there, and soon people were faced with starvation. For the next six months, people survived off the leaves and wild fruits, which then were named "riath waak" (plentiful), and fish from the Raad River. The government of Sudan wouldn't allow the International Committee of the Red CROSS (ICRC) to bring in food. Both sides were in protracted negotiations while the refugees were dying of starvation and diseases in the camp.

After months of negotiations, however, Sudan's government allowed the ICRC to deliver food to refugees. It was too late for many.

After a few weeks of food distribution in the camp, the same government of Sudan, which had allowed the ICRC to deliver food to refugees, sent in its army to attack the camp. The Sudan Armed Forces (SAF), with the local allied militia, attacked the camp from all directions and overran the town, killing many innocent refugees. We now found ourselves back on our feet, beginning a new journey in the path of terror. Everybody just ran without carrying anything, and the challenges were unbearable along the way. People were being ambushed and fired upon by the SAF and their allied militias. People were being killed like herds of animals that had fallen into the ambush of hunters. Many were dying of starvation and dehydration. There was no food or water, no sleep or rest. It was a tough situation, worse than my journey to Ethiopia. I was sure I was going to die, but it was just a matter of when.

After three weeks, our group arrived in Kapoeta town in Eastern Equatoria State. This town was controlled by the SPLA, and they received us warmly. They fed us for a few days while those who had sustained light wounds were treated for their injuries. It was tough to carry those with major injuries because we were under constant attack. Those who were wounded badly were left behind to die. Everybody was fighting for his or her own life.

In Kapoeta, things were not right either. The Sudan Air Force had been dropping bombs on the town day and night. There were rumours that SAF was advancing on the ground from all directions. It was a tough time for the SPLA as the rebel movement had divided itself into two factions in a 1991 rebellion. Riek Machar, Lam Akol and Gordon Kong had broken away from the mainstream SPLA and formed what was known as SPLM/A-Nasir, and left SPLM/A for John Garang and his followers.

Now, the SPLA mainstream was fighting both the SPLM/A faction and the real enemy, the regime in Khartoum. Many towns that were once liberated by the SPLA were now retaken by SAF, including Garang's hometown Bor and civilians in rural areas and in cattle camps were massacred by Riek's White Army and his troops. The survivors from the Bor massacre sought refuge in Internally Displaced Persons Camps (IDPCs) in southern Sudan or in refugee camps in neighbouring Uganda or DR Congo.

With news of the constant air attacks and of the enemy approaching from all fronts, everybody was anxious about what was going to happen. I was worried because I didn't know where else the people would go. Kapoeta was the only safe place for other refugees and me because the SPLA was there and could protect us. It appeared to us that the town would soon fall to the enemy if an attack took place. The SPLA seemed outnumbered and outgunned, while the enemy would come in equipped with any tools to flush it out of the town. It was our second day in town, and our ears were already full of this rumour.

In our first two days, there was a lull in the bombing, which was an unusual thing for the town that had been under constant bombing for the last two months. However, on the third day, the bombing was very intense, and many people were killed. The bombing that was carried out by three Sudanese warplanes started in the morning and continued for the whole day. Everything in town was in smoke and flames. The bombing continued throughout the night. The following morning, the SPLA was battling SAF just a few kilometres away from town. The local militia, which did not like the SPLA presence on their soil, allied themselves with the enemy and joined the attack on the SPLA from the rear. The SPLA had already lost a good number of its forces, and they were pushed back to the town by intense shelling and bombings from the enemy's artilleries and warplanes. They were being squeezed from all directions. The SPLA was fighting a losing battle, and very soon, the town was overrun and captured by the SAF.

This gave the SAF the upper hand to intensify its bombing and killings as people fled the town.

Again, we were forced to flee for safety, but this time it was worse. The militia was waiting on the edge of town. It was chaos as everybody was frantically fleeing to save their lives. Many older persons and children were left behind in the aftermath. It was a terrible exodus. Thousands of people were trying to escape an imminent death on a massive scale while it was too late for others.

The enemy was bombing people as they fled, and many were torn into pieces as a result.

SAF allied militia took advantage of the SAF's defeat of the SPLA by ambushing and killing people as they escaped. These killings continued for more than two weeks. The remnants of the SPLA soldiers who joined the fleeing civilians tried to fight off the militia, but still, many innocent lives were lost. More precious lives were lost to dehydration as there was no water along the way.

I was confused and didn't know where people were heading. I was tired, hungry and worried about the militia's bullets. I had blisters on my feet that bled with every step. Most of the time, I felt as if I were dead, but something pushed me to move on. It had been almost five years since I last saw my family. I was now fourteen years old. My hope for finding them just about ended. I rarely thought of them. Instead, I thought only of how to survive.

I arrived at a small outpost called Key Base. I saw the SPLA soldiers that were fleeing with us being disarmed by Kenyan police as they crossed the border. Seeing this happening, I was worried and feared death ahead because I had never trusted any other armed men apart from the SPLA soldiers who had fought bravely with militias and averted what could have been terrible bloodbaths. "Now they are disarmed. Who will protect us?" I asked myself.

Now people were moving along with the SPLA disarmed soldiers, and I followed. There was nothing I could do but follow everybody.

After a walk of a few kilometres, we arrived at a Kenya border point where a huge UN water tank was stationed to provide water to people. The UN staff then distributed food, giving us life after days of starvation. We were in Lokichogio, a Kenyan border town, I was told. We spent about two months there while more and more refugees were still coming in. The UN was feeding us and helping with medical care. We were then transported to Kakuma, just two hours from Lokichogio, where a huge refugee camp was established. We were being trucked in, my first time travelling in a vehicle since being separated from my family. We were registered and given a new identity as refugees. We were each given a ration card that we could use to access food, medicine, and education.

After a nearly five-year struggle to survive, I arrived more dead than alive at the refugee camp in Kakuma, Kenya. It was the latter part of 1992. Although I continued to think about my parents, brothers and sister day and night, I resigned myself to never seeing them again. Instead, I prayed fervently for their safety wherever they may have gone.

My life before the war

In the mid-1970s, my parents were married in the small town of Akot in Lakes State in the formerly southern Sudan. My mom came from the nearby village of Agany and lived with her childhood friend, Aluel, who married a northern merchant. Aluel wanted my mom to live with her during her first year of marriage.

Aluel's husband, Aramiden, had also married my aunt, Yar Maguen, as his first wife after he migrated to Akot several years earlier. Polygamy was an integral part of our traditional culture in Sudan and allowed by law.

My father learned his business skills from Aramiden and later started his own successful commodities business in the village of Akot. He sold clothes, food, medicine, and many other things the locals needed. He would consult with Aramiden while visiting with his sister's family. During those visits, my mom was always there and would provide him with cool water and food. She was a young, attractive girl who was always busy pounding grain, fetching firewood or water from a distance and cooking meals twice a day.

When my dad was ready to get married, my Aunt Yar recommended my mom as a wife for him because she was a hard-working and honest girl. In Dinka culture, marriage is decided by the bridegroom's family members. A wife can be chosen by any member of the family or by a friend based on her respect, hard work, and social status. The groom's family would then propose the idea of marriage to the prospective bride's family, who, if interested, would determine the number of cows they require in exchange for their daughter. When both sides agree on the bargain, the marriage is concluded, and the bride moves to her husband. My parents were married according to this customary Dinka process and not in a church.

After their marriage, my parents moved to Rumbek, where my dad ran his business. I was born there at my Aunt Temnaam Manyiel's house on a Saturday, but the date and year of my birth were not recorded. My aunt was a midwife and delivered me at her home. I was given the name Sabit, which in Arabic means someone born on Saturday.

When I was about eight years old, my name was changed to Maker, which means a white and black spotted bull, because there was a Maker bull in my father's dowry. My father's name is Mabor, which means all-white bull, while his father's name is Marial, which means a bull that is black but has white spots on both sides of its belly. All my names reflect the colours of bulls

– Maker Mabor Marial.

My parents both grew up during the first civil war between the north and the southern rebel movement known as Anya-Nya One (snake venom). The war broke out just as the British were preparing to leave Sudan to give people their independence. During this process, most of the power was left in the hands of the northern Arabs, which left the people of southern Sudan feeling unsafe. War broke out in 1955, one year before Sudan gained its independence. At that time, there was no education system in southern Sudan. Consequently, my parents didn't get a chance to go to school; they were left uneducated and remained illiterate. That civil war continued for 17 years until it ended with a peace agreement signed in Addis Ababa, Ethiopia, in 1972. In that agreement, southern Sudan was granted an autonomous administration.

Though my parents were illiterate, my father became a successful businessman, and my mom helped him run the business. Their life was good. My father was the provider for all the relatives. People would come to our house for everything: food, clothing, medicine, and comfort. Even those who were not related to us would come to our house for their needs.

After a while, my family moved: first back to Akot for business reasons and then to Karic, which was just a few miles away. In Karic, my dad's business became even more successful. My father also got involved in farming. He grew peanuts and sorghum and raised livestock such as goats and cattle.

When I turned five, I was helping my parents in goat herding near the house. I started my education then, one year early, which was rare in Sudan at the time. This came about when my childhood friend Makol Akec (RIP) encouraged me to start going to school with him. He would go to school in the morning, and in the afternoon, he would herd goats with me. He always took his books with him. While in the grazing area, when goats were deep in their grazing, Makol would open his books and begin to read quietly or sometimes out loud. He taught me how to read the alphabet in Arabic because Arabic was the language of instruction in Sudan then.

Every morning, I would see him going to school dressed in white cotton shorts and a shirt. It was a tradition for primary school pupils to dress all in white back then. Makol would always have his white cotton school backpack filled with textbooks and exercise books. He looked very impressive to me, and I could not wait to turn six, so I could be officially admitted to a school.

While I was still five, Makol told me that since I was so interested in learning, I should go with him to school the next day. He said that the old headmaster was a kindly man that would not refuse a student with a desire to learn. I was excited about the possibility of starting school and agreed to go with him. The next morning, I dressed neatly in my regular clothes and waited eagerly for Makol outside. He showed up, and together we went to school. It was a great day for me. I was excited and hopeful to be admitted as one of the pupils.

When we arrived at school, my friend joined his class, leaving me to sit under a tree, waiting for the headmaster to come and enrol me in his class. When the headmaster came to teach his first-year class, I went to him very excitedly and asked if he could allow me to be in his class. The first thing he asked was my age. I said that I was five, and he said, "Five is not the legal age for a child to start school in Sudan." He used his thick classroom ruler to measure my height and concluded that I should wait until the following year to enrol.

I spent the rest of that morning and the afternoon crying until my friend came home from school. He found me sitting behind our shop, looking sad. He asked, "What happened, Sabit?" I didn't respond right away. I paused for a while and then said, "The headmaster told me I was too young to be enrolled, and therefore, he could not enrol me in his first-year class. That is why I'm very sad and unhappy." In sympathy, my friend asked if I would go home with him, and I agreed. He was in his third grade at Karic Primary School. His sister Adak Akec (RIP), a dedicated young lady with outstanding academic records, was in fifth grade.

Adak was among the few girls allowed to have that rare opportunity for a very limited education. The Dinka culture held that school-educated girls end up marrying those their parents do not like or getting pregnant while still in school. At their house, we were served *cuin/kuin atac* (fortified porridge) with peanuts and goat milk. It was cold and fresh. It looked like mashed potato and was delicious.

After we ate, my friend gave me friendly advice. In Dinka culture, there is a saying: "Let his age-mate teach him." This means that young people get great advice from their age-mates or peer groups, the kind of advice that parents cannot give to their children. He encouraged me to keep going to school and to continue to sit under the tree next to the tree where the class was held. In those days, most classes in southern Sudan were held outdoors, under trees, because the Anya-Nya One war had just ended, leaving no infrastructure or development in the southern part of the country. This left an educational system without essentials.

My friend advised me that by sitting under the tree next to the one that served as our local classroom, I would have a chance to see the blackboard, which was usually placed on two very high poles leaning against the tree. I would also hear the instructor clearly, being so close. This sounded to me like a great idea. The following morning, I woke up earlier than everybody else in the house. I brushed my teeth, took a shower, combed my hair, and got dressed. It was a trial, but I was excited about it. I went outside and waited for Makol to come. A few minutes later, he showed up, and we went to school together.

After we arrived in the school compound, my friend went straight to join his class in the general assembly. In Sudan, pupils congregate in a designated area every morning. This is called the general assembly or the parade. It is where the roll call is taken, absences are reported, and morning devotions are conducted. Pupils are also checked for hygiene and punished if they come wearing dirty clothes, dirty or uncombed hair, and for previous absences or tardiness.

After the assembly, pupils were sent to their respective classrooms, including that first-year class that I earnestly wanted to join. The pupils came first while the teacher was still in his office preparing for the lesson. When pupils came to the class, they were excited to see me sitting under a nearby tree. They thought that I was admitted as their new classmate. Some even offered to share their bench with me. Most of these pupils come from Karic, my village, and we would play together after school. They were upset when they learned that I was not officially admitted as a pupil in the school.

Soon their math teacher appeared, and the pupils stood up to welcome him. He said in Arabic, "saba ker talaba." (Good morning, pupils), and the pupils responded, "saba ker ustaz" (good morning, teacher.) I did the same, and the teacher looked at me standing alone under the tree but didn't say anything. He then took his chalk and, on the far right of the blackboard, wrote the date, 10/04/1982, and then in the middle, he wrote the subject, Math, with double lines under it. He then turned to his pupils and asked them if anyone could still remember the lesson for the previous day. Some pupils raised their hands, saying, "anna, anna, anna," Arabic for "me, me, me." The teacher picked my friend Kau Adut, and Kau started counting the numbers correctly from one through ten in Arabic. After he finished, the teacher said, "thapak aa lo," which means clap for him. Then the teacher started his lesson for the day by introducing additional numbers from eleven through twenty. After his lesson, he left, and the Arabic teacher came to instruct us.

After this second lesson, there was a break, and the pupils went to the field for fifteen minutes to play or eat snacks, mostly peanuts they had brought with them from their homes. After ten minutes, the bell rang, and everybody went back to class. The classes went on until it was noon. Another bell rang, this one for lunch. My friend invited me to join him at the school dining service. The food that was made from sorghum and known as asida in Arabic or cuin/kuin in Dinka was served in a big bowl. The soup was made of dried fish with vegetables and was served in a separate bowl. Five pupils would share a bowl. There were no spoons provided; each pupil had to bring his or her own spoon from home. I didn't have mine, but my friend had planned for us to have lunch together and had brought with him an extra spoon. In this school canteen, there was always enough food for the pupils and even for the children in the village who were not enrolled in school.

After an hour's lunch break, the bell rang, and the pupils went back to their classes. I left to sit alone under the nearby tree. Five minutes later, the headmaster came to teach the class. During this class period, he would teach Dinka, my native dialect or religion, which was Christianity. That day he came to teach religion, and he began to talk about creation. It was all in Dinka, and I could understand every single word of it. It was amazing to me to learn that there was a being who created the universe, living and non-living things, human beings, and animals. That day was the day I really came to understand God, the "Maker of Heaven and Earth". After his lesson, the headmaster left, and the music teacher came in. He started by asking pupils to sing the last song they had sung before the class ended the day before. The pupils sang, and I could feel the excitement from my isolation under the nearby tree. The pupils were singing while slapping on their books and backpacks. It was a fun lesson. At the end of his period, the teacher left, and the last bell rang, which meant everybody was going home. My friend and I walked home together. It was a great day.

For a year, I would go every morning, sit quietly under my lonely tree, and learn on my own. The knowledge I was gaining illegally was still knowledge. I was learning like every other pupil in the class. I was doing my homework and learning the songs. I went to school every day until the following year when the headmaster Akim, allowed me to enrol officially as a pupil.

The headmaster decided that since I had been listening in to the classes for two terms, I should be tested to see what I had learned, like with the regular pupils. This was great news for me. I took the final exams and passed, standing number four out of more than 100 pupils. It was a surprise to many pupils and other people in the school as well as in the village. In Sudan and Africa as a whole, the community would usually be invited to witness a school's announcement of final examination results. This day was a big day for me because my parents were there to witness my success. When I got home, I got many gifts, which included new clothes and shoes. As a result of this success, I waited excitedly for the next year as the new pupil, who would be wearing the white school uniform and having a school bag full of books and pencils while being a second-year pupil.

During the long break between school years, there were many other activities I enjoyed with my friends in the village, including moulding cows and other animal toys out of clay soil and making shields of palm leaves and using them for defence during stone fights. During that time, children from my village and nearby villages would gather at one designated area where they would divide up into two groups that would fiercely fight each other. They would throw stones at each other, and the shields would be used for defence from being injured. Traditionally, this was a way for children to learn how to become warriors who could fight bravely, defending cows and people in the village. With all these activities to occupy my time, the school break seemed very short. April was approaching so quickly. It was the time when all the schools in Sudan would open.

With school opening just around the corner, I had another problem. My sister Nyankaric was sick. She suffered from a mysterious illness, and the nerves in her neck were badly affected. She could not sit by herself, turn her neck around or walk. Her illness progressed so quickly that within a few days, she was completely bedridden. Her arms were getting thinner and thinner, and she could not even handle a spoon. At that point, she was in a complete vegetative state. Her condition was getting worse and worse. My dad and mom started taking her to different hospitals between Rumbek, Akot and Yirol with no improvement at all. My brother Akot and I were left with relatives, mainly our Aunt Anger. She was a good caretaker, but since she was so young, her role was limited to the family home affairs and not outside matters such as school.

Pupils were buying their textbooks, exercise books, pens, pencils, and uniforms in the days leading to the school's opening. Every day, I would see some of my close friends bringing home their school supplies and uniforms, but I was waiting for my parents, who were still attending to my ailing sister in the hospital. Without my sister's illness, school supplies and uniforms would have been simple things for my parents to get for me because they were financially stable. With no improvement in my sister's condition, my parents did not come home until two weeks into April. As a result, when it was time for school to begin, I didn't have my uniform or school supplies. I decided that not having a uniform would not prevent me from going to school that day. I woke up early, got cleaned and dressed in my normal clothes.

The school's head teacher, Samuel, was one in charge of welcoming pupils back to school. He was checking every individual pupil for cleanliness and making sure no one was wearing an old uniform from last year. When he came to me, he was shocked at what he saw and paused for a moment without saying anything. He directed his square face, with narrowed red eyes and a flat nose, toward me. I knew that I was in big trouble but just didn't know how to react. He was well-known for being a teacher of radical brutality toward his pupils. Filled with fear, I began to shiver. I looked scared and started to cry. That didn't give him compassion. Instead, he opened his mouth, revealing a few teeth sticking out of red gums, and said, "Where is your uniform, boy?" I said I didn't have one, and he said, "Why are you here then?" I responded, "My father is in Rumbek, and he will bring my uniform tomorrow." However, this did not convince him, and he said, "I want you to go home until the day you have your uniform on." I didn't say anything, and my only motion was the tears rolling down my small cheeks. I didn't want to be sent home because of not having my school uniform on. I didn't want to leave at all. The teacher looked at me several times to see if I was leaving, but I was still there. "Go, or I will do this," he said, and he was waving in the air his three-foot-long whip made from hippo's skin. It was made for whipping pupils who disobey the teachers, including him. In Sudan, teachers would punish their pupils by lashing them up to 25 times or more, depending on the seriousness of the violation. And mine was one of the more serious violations, punishable by several lashes ranging from five to ten.

Samuel turned to me and said, "Are you still here, boy? His voice grew louder and louder, "Leave, leave the school compound." He was walking toward me, but I didn't want to leave. His first strike landed on my head and reached the middle of my back. It felt as if it a bolt had fallen from the sky. All my body's nerves were electrified. I fell to the ground. Samuel kept lashing my small body. It was painful, and I was nearly unconscious. The clothes I had on, shorts and shirt, were already ripped apart, and their pieces were flying. There was blood everywhere. I cried until I ran out of tears, but his heart had no mercy. Samuel continued beating me until he became tired. Then he resorted to another even more painful and humiliating punishment. He asked all the pupils to repeat after him, "He is naked; we see his penis, oh, oh, Oooh. He is naked; we see his penis, oh, oh, Oooh, oh." This went on for about fifteen minutes, and the whole village was clouded by the noise from the school. The day that I had hoped would be one of the best of my life had become this.

Later that night, my father came from Rumbek after getting the news from a cyclist who had left in the morning when the incident was still taking place. My father was very upset and, at first, wanted to confront the head teacher, but he soon calmed down and decided only to seek some medical care for me. I remained in critical condition for the next few weeks and could not go to school. Meanwhile, my dad bought me two pairs of uniforms, while many parents could barely afford one.

After I recovered from the beating, I went back to school dressed as clean and neat as every other pupil. Despite being away for weeks, I was soon very competitive in the class. The first term, I stood number three out of more than 100 pupils. I continued to be in the top five during the next years. Even Samuel, a man who tried to discourage me from my dream of education, gave me special presents during announcements of the examination results. From these early years in my village, my dream of an education was nurtured, and the injustices that I often witnessed in my youth fueled my desire to be a lawyer one day. One day, I hoped to be the voice for the weaker and smaller members of society.

My Years in the Middle of Nowhere

Kakuma in Swahili means "nowhere", which was an appropriate name for the place where I would spend much of my adolescence. The Kakuma Refugee Camp is located in the middle of a semi-arid desert with a challenging environment for human habitation. The United Nations High Commissioner for Refugees (UNHCR) established Kakuma Refugee Camp in 1992 in response to the then-massive influx of Sudanese refugees who were being forced out of their homes by the civil war. I arrived in 1992 at the conclusion of my own long, dangerous journey. The camp gradually expanded to serve other refugees fleeing from Somalia, Ethiopia, Burundi, the Democratic Republic of Congo, Eritrea, Uganda and Rwanda. By the end of 2000, the refugee population at Kakuma had grown to 230,000 refugees, the majority of whom came from Somalia and Sudan.

Just beyond the borders of the refugee camp lived the Turkana tribe. The Turkana people of Kenya keep cattle, goats, donkeys, and camels. Cattle rustling was common in the Turkana district and around its borders with Uganda, South Sudan and Ethiopia. Turkana people were often involved in fights over livestock and water control. One of the traditional practices by Turkana tribesmen is the tattooing of men or warriors who killed enemies to indicate what they have done for the community.

The UNHCR ran the Kakuma Refugee Camp in collaboration with other organizations such as the World Food Program (WFP), International Organization for Migration (IOM), Lutheran World Federation (LWF), International Rescue Committee (IRC), Jesuit Refugee Services (JRS), National Council of Churches of Kenya, Windle Trust Kenya, Film Aid International, and Salesians of Don Bosco in Kenya.

The Kakuma Refugee Camp looked like a tiny metropolis. It had thousands of thatched roof huts or tukuls, tents and mud houses. The UN provided the materials while refugees built the huts themselves.

Building our own housing was not a problem for us. Many knew from home and from the camp in Ethiopia how to build and maintain them. Our main concern was always the materials, which the UN supplied only once every three years.

If the thatched roof on your tukul was eaten away by the termites or collapsed for some reason before three years passed, you were on your own. You could sell a portion of your 14-day food rations many times to buy these materials or stay under a roofless tukul until the next cycle of distribution of construction materials. There was some assistance in these kinds of situations, though, but it was time-consuming to pursue, and often your application would not be approved after months or even years of follow-ups.

When you arrived as a refugee at the border town of Lokichogio or at any other ports of entry, you endured a long registration process. You were booked, and medically checked before being transported to the camp where you be given a ration card, cooking utensils, and sleeping materials. When you were finally admitted into the camp, it was not easy to ever leave the camp without getting travel documents from camp authorities. Refugees were required to obtain their passes from UNHCR and the Kenyan Government before they could travel. This process was always long with many strings attached, and you might ultimately be denied a pass and remain stuck there.

Kakuma Refugee Camp was not a welcoming place. The local Turkana villagers were heavily armed, and some would come to the camp to rob people at night. The camp was so crowded that water sources and food distribution centres were major sources of conflict. Fighting would start between two people and escalate to engulf the whole camp, and unfortunately, many innocent people would die.

The way the camp was set up resulted in many conflicts. People were grouped together based on their origins, tribes, ethnicities, clans or even by families. In the event one person from a particular group had a problem with someone from another, both communities would become involved in a fierce fight. This made movement from place to place more difficult in the camp. Those who did not know about the problem most often fell victim when their communities had a fight with others while away and would unexpectedly find themselves in the middle of a fight after their return.

Diseases such as cholera and malaria were deadly in the camp. An outbreak would spread quickly because of the density of the population. In July of 1997, cholera started in the Somali community, spread quickly to our Sudanese group, and killed one of my neighbours within a few hours.

The camp environment was harsh. It was always hot, windy, and dusty during the day. Classes were cancelled occasionally due to dust storms when dust filled the exercise books, and students could not write. The average daily temperature often reached 40 degrees Celsius, or 104 degrees Fahrenheit.

In addition, the camp was infested with scorpions, snakes and poisonous spiders. Scorpions killed people with a single sting or left them paralyzed and in excruciating pain for several days.

Due to its semi-arid climate, Kakuma is ill-suited for agriculture. Locals could only make a living on their livestock and the few trees they cut down for charcoal that they sold to refugees. Refugees were largely dependent on UN handouts. There were very few paying jobs, and the few who got jobs with the UN were poorly paid.

This kind of environment made the locals hostile to refugees, particularly when they saw refugees being given food while they were not. For this reason, robberies in the camp at night were rampant, and many refugees were murdered. There were also bandits on the routes between Lokichogio and Kakuma, Kakuma to Lodwar. This hostility made travelling by land in northern Kenya dangerous and with a high risk of ambush by Turkana bandits. My cousin Makuac Mabor was killed on the way from Lokichogio to Nerus in southern Sudan in 1999 in an ambush laid by Turkana bandits. It was one of several events that convinced me that I did not want to spend much time there.

Throughout the years I spent in Kakuma, the relationship between Turkana tribesmen and refugees deteriorated as life for the local Turkana community became even more desperate. Turkana tribesmen were turning their guns against the helpless refugees and killing many of them. A series of ghastly attacks started erupting after 1994 when the first refugee was shot and killed. The intensifying hostilities ultimately resulted in an all-out war between the Turkana tribesmen and the Sudanese refugees in June 2003. Many people from both sides were killed.

In Kakuma, there were 23 primary schools and three secondary schools built by the United Nations for the refugees' kids. Any kid who could balance the demands of school with the hardships of the camp was encouraged by the UN to complete an education. I took that opportunity seriously with a single goal in mind, to finish my secondary schooling, go back to southern Sudan, volunteer in the Sudan People's Liberation Army (SPLA), fight against the regime in Khartoum and liberate my people from oppression.

With a secondary school education, I believed I could make a good military officer. Most SPLA officers joined the movement before completing their primary education. While some had never been to school in their life. It would have been beneficial to them, I reasoned, to have someone in their ranks with a secondary school certificate.

I immersed myself fully in my studies in Kakuma. My first goal was to finish my primary school education. I had an English grammar teacher there named James who inspired in me an enthusiasm for learning the English language. My math teacher, Hamza, a refugee from Ethiopia, taught with passion and professionalism, which also made me love his class.

After I graduated from primary school, I continued to pursue my studies. In secondary school, I had another excellent English teacher named Kenyi. I took classes in geography, religion, history and government, scoring A's in all of them. In sciences such as physics, biology, and chemistry, I was getting average scores. I performed poorly in Swahili and math.

The headmaster at Napata Secondary, named Laurence, was a great man with outstanding leadership skills. He was a Kenyan and had been a headmaster for 19 years before being hired as our school headmaster. I loved him because he had a great heart for Sudanese refugees and always understood the fact that Southern Sudanese had been marginalized educationally for generations. For this reason, he wanted to contribute toward training his African brothers and sisters to become leaders who would rebuild their country and take it in the right direction.

I looked forward to morning devotion at our school each day; it brought everybody together regardless of their separate beliefs. Our school also offered clubs that we could participate in, such as journalism, debate, sports, and drama. My favourites were the drama and journalism clubs.

At 10:00 a.m., some women in the camp would serve a sugarless porridge to all of the students. We would line up in front of the kitchen and receive our portion. The few students who had money could buy a packet of sugar to mix in their porridge.

Although I was on the path to securing my secondary certificate during my long years at Kakuma, I gave up my hope for a college education. My dreams of becoming a lawyer were dashed against the harsh realities of my current state.

The Resettlement Process

In 1998, there were rumours that the unaccompanied minors were to be resettled in the U.S., and the group caseworkers were preparing their lists for submission to the UNHCR for the resettlement program. Americans were coming to the camp and holding group meetings to tell people how to prepare for their interviews. It was an exciting time.

After years of waiting and merely surviving, I was beginning to think perhaps God had been strengthening and preparing me for this opportunity to go to the U.S., where I would be able to finish my education and return home to help my people. I did not have to wait for the interviews for long. I was sitting in our compound one evening when John Ater Dhieu, who lived with me in the same compound and worked for the UNHCR as an interpreter, came with the lists containing the names of unaccompanied minors. My cousin Mabior Achol Majok, also known as Adomic, was on the list. The following morning, he went for his first interview. He was asked for the names of those he wanted to be grouped with. Accordingly, my cousin Adomic added Peter Majang, Maker Jok, and myself to his form. He did not tell us about this until the night before a second interview which we were all scheduled to attend. The four of us went to that interview on August 24, 2000. This was one of the first few interviews conducted by the UNHCR to determine the eligibility of individual applicants for relocation to a third country. At this stage, the individual applicants were asked to say who they were, what made them refugees and why they wanted to be resettled in a third country. The whole idea for this interview was for the UNHCR to prove to the third country that it had selected refugees appropriately.

At this stage, some refugees who failed to tell their stories honestly were rejected. For us, everything went smoothly on the first day, and our case was approved for further consideration by the U.S. Embassy and immigration officials.

A few days later, our names appeared on the billboard with the names of 100 other refugees scheduled for an interview with United States immigration officials. It was a great development for the four of us. We attended the interview where immigration officials had to make sure that everything, including our names and ages, was correct. After that, we were scheduled for further interviews with the Immigration and Naturalization Service (INS), a part of the U.S. immigration office that determines the eligibility of a refugee for relocation to the U.S. Many people were denied entry after this intense scrutiny.

We did the INS interview and waited nervously for the result for two weeks. Our hearts were pumping all the time heavily. We weren't sure whether we would be accepted or not. However, one evening, a friend of mine told me that he saw our names on the list of those whose INS results were out. We were invited to go to the UN Compound in the morning and collect our letters. I was excited, though still nervous. I took a flashlight and went to the billboard to check whether what I was told was true. They were there, and I excitedly returned home and informed the rest. The next morning, we went to the UN Compound and collected our INS results. We were shaking as we entered the room and people looked through the file of letters after receiving your name. It was a common belief that those who received thick and heavy envelopes were those accepted, and those given thin and light envelopes were those rejected. Ours were thick and heavy, so we assumed that we were accepted even though we did not open the envelopes and read their contents. We passed our interviews, and we were excited. Now our next step in the process was the International Organization for Immigration (IOM), where our medical check would be done and travel arrangements made. We went through the whole process and were ready to leave for the U.S. in one month. Many refugees had to wait as many as four years to be finally resettled in the U.S. or in any other third country.

We then became part of the first 102 Lost Boys and Girls accepted to fly to the U.S. We left on November 26, 2000, just weeks after receiving our acceptance letters from the INS.

I was so excited – I could fulfil my dreams of higher education and extend a helping hand to those left behind in Africa.

Despite the fact that I was excruciatingly poor, I tried hard to organize a big farewell party and invite many people in my community and from other neighbouring communities to come and celebrate my departure and the beginning of my new life in the United States.

I woke up on the morning of November 26, 2000, with eager anticipation but realised that I would be separated from my people, the people with whom I had lived for many years, whose love and smiles kept me alive and helped me overcome all odds. However, I said to myself that there was nothing I could do but move on. My only hope was that the people I cared about would come to the U.S., too, so we could meet again. I packed my small bag with a few of my belongings and left most behind for others to use.

That afternoon, an aeroplane landed on Kakuma's dirt runway, and 40 of us, including Somalis and other refugees, were herded into UN trucks and rushed to the airstrip, where we said goodbye to Kakuma Camp and its people. It was a special moment but difficult at the same time. We were leaving behind our friends, teachers, brothers, sisters, and communities that encompassed all kinds of people, including the local Turkana people. My journey would continue even further away from Sudan.

After bidding our final farewell through the small windows of the plane, we were on the way to our destination. Our first stop was at Jomo Kenyatta Airport in Nairobi, Kenya, where we found food and warm clothing ready for us. It would take us an entire day with a few stops on our way to get to the United States of America, a country that was made famous among the refugees through products stamped with "Gift from the American People."

When we arrived at JFK airport in New York, we were split and put on different planes destined for different cities across the U.S. Only 6 of us were destined for Virginia. We were told in our cultural orientation in Kakuma that we would be distributed to all 50 U.S. states except Alaska due to its extreme weather conditions. Even though no one among us had been to the U.S. before, many of us expected good things from America: a better life, better education, and better jobs. There was a lot of optimism for a brighter future, even if we would only be a few among many strangers and could not have our longtime friends with us.

Richmond, Virginia, USA

On the night of November 27, 2000, volunteers from Refugee and Immigration Services and Catholic Charities met us at Richmond International Airport. It was a chilly night with a slight breeze blowing through the clear air. It was very cold to us because we were accustomed to the hot climate of Turkana District. The volunteers held balloons that said "welcome." We were humbled by the warm welcome at the airport by people we did not know. They were all white but appeared happy to receive us. Our initial assumption was that everybody would be rude to us in America since nobody wanted to talk to us on the plane and at the airport after our arrival. Everybody we saw was busy and did not want to answer whatever questions we posed in our broken English.

Now our group was split into two. Maker Abraham Jok and Elijah Alier Anyieth, who were both 17 years old, were taken to the Children's Home of Virginia Baptist in Petersburg, Virginia. While Peter Magok Majang, Kuol Anyieth and I were taken to Midlothian, Virginia, and placed in a temporary house. This house had already been prepared for some Congolese refugees, but their trip had to be delayed because a new baby was born to the couple in the camp and new paperwork had to be refiled with the U.S. Immigration and Naturalization Service (INS).

The two volunteers who met us at the airport brought us to our first home in the U.S. They quickly oriented us on how to turn the lights on and off and work the stove, shower, and flush the toilet. They showed us the refrigerator, which had our food, and our bedrooms. This orientation was quick, with too much information to be absorbed in less than 30 minutes. We were also shown how to use the telephone in case of an emergency.

When the volunteers departed, we were left alone in the big house, unlike our tukuls in the Kakuma Refugee Camp. The three of us spent the night in a neighbourhood where we did not know anybody. We were fearful and afraid of the unknown, and my roommates suggested we all sleep in one room, but I refused. Our greatest fear was for criminals because, in Kakuma, we were told that armed criminals in America would attack people in their homes to rob or kill them. We watched many violent American movies in Kakuma, and we thought that was the culture. So, we were fearful that we would be attacked by criminals who might have seen us as new people in the neighbourhood.

Despite the welcome at the airport and our initial view of the country, the adjustment to our new lives would not be easy. We had already had a taste of this before we got to Richmond during a layover in New York. Upon our arrival at JFK International Airport, we immediately faced the challenges of a language barrier. Even though we had studied English, we could not understand many people at the airport. The employees there tried to talk to us, but we could not understand them. They spoke so fast and used so many words we could not comprehend. When it became clear that we could get nowhere in our direct communication, the airport officials decided to give us nametags with our full names and the addresses of our final destinations. This made it easy for the employees to know where we were going and direct us to the right planes. This reminded me of what the Education Coordinator at Kakuma Refugee Camp, Mr Maker Thiong Maal, had told us at our farewell ceremony organized by the community leaders. In his speech, Mr Maal said, "Now you are going to the United States, a new country with a different culture, and there are a lot of things you may not understand. One thing among these is the language barrier. Though many of you claim here that you know English, American English is different and difficult. Many of you may not understand it for a number of years." His message proved true at the airport.

It was very quiet in the neighbourhood because the neighbours were already asleep. It was very cold, 55 degrees, and nearly freezing to us, the newly arrived African refugees. We had no idea how to work the heating system to warm up the house. Peter and Kuol were sleeping in what was planned to be the children's room, and I was in the family room. My room was quite big and empty. This was the first time for me to be in a room alone after many years of being in a refugee camp. There, people lived close together. I had people around me all the time - youths, elders, and women - they all had a role in looking out for each other.

There were so many concerns in my mind that night: Would I be in a community where everybody cares for the welfare of others? Would I find friends? Would people in the community be kind to us? Would we be victims of crimes? Every elder in the camp warned us about crime in the US. We were repeatedly told that in the United States, everybody could buy a gun from the local store. "Criminals who rob other people in their homes sometimes use these guns," we were told. For this reason, the night and the following morning were rough. We felt alone and seemed to have completely lost our community ties. We thought criminals would just roam in the community at night and would attack anybody in their homes. We just imagine that they would be taping on the boards and doors and ordering us to give them what we didn't have.

To make this worse, in the middle of the night, as we had just fallen asleep, the alarm clock went off. The three of us didn't know what it was. We thought our house was on fire! We rushed out of our bedrooms in our pyjamas to the living room to investigate. We looked at the alarm clock, but no one could figure it out. We were confused about the little thing. Eventually, I took a closer look and saw an on and off button. I pushed it to the offside, and the misery ended.

The next morning, we got up early and tried to go outside in the hope of acquainting ourselves with the neighbours, but we could only see people passing by in their cars. There were no people around; people were either inside, in their cars, or at work. As we looked around the community, we could see only white people. No African Americans or Sudanese. This was a major concern to us because in our Dinka culture, or Africa as a whole, a tribe lives in a village close together, and the tribe members see each other every day and ask about each other's welfare. In our new community, only a few would say "Hi," and even from a distance. No handshakes or inquiries about who we were and where we came from.

Three days after being in this strange neighbourhood and inside the house, most of the time, because of the cold, we decided to go out. We were bored and tired, and we were not used to being in one place for many hours at a time, let alone days. In the camp, we would visit friends or play during our free time. This was a difficult time for us. While we were outside, Kuol and I decided to go to a nearby convenience store to buy soda and a newspaper. Bill, our landlord, had given us each $5 the day before as a way for us to be acquainted with American money. The store was not far, and we came back in less than 20 minutes.

While we were gone, Peter, whom we had left standing in front of the house, took a bike from the house and rode it around in the street. We saw him on the bike from a distance, and I could not wait to ride it. As we reached the house, I asked Peter if I could ride the bike, and he said, "Sure." He gave it to me, and I took a ride. I left Peter standing there while Kuol took our groceries inside. I made several circles in the neighbourhood and returned to the house. The ride was fun, and I loved it. Once inside, Kuol and I were sitting in the kitchen and writing letters to let friends and relatives we left in the refugee camp know about our safe arrival. It was a beautiful afternoon despite being chilly outside. Peter, our roommate, was sitting on the sofa in the living room, watching our small TV. It was a good day as we were starting to feel the sense of the good American life.

Soon, all that changed. Within a few minutes, we heard frightening news from Peter: cars with armed men were pulling up in front of our house. People were getting out with guns drawn and taking position behind trees, near doors and all the windows around our house. I said, "Peter, don't be lying to us," and he said, "Come and see for yourself." I rushed to the living room and looked through the blinds, and to my surprise, the gun was right at my face. I ran back to the kitchen and looked through the window, and again there was a gun at my face. We were under siege! We knew that we were going to die in just a matter of minutes. As the situation grew tenser, Peter took a leadership role. He said, "Come guys and sit down here and let them come in and kill us while sitting. They will be asked later why they killed people sitting in their living room." Peter said these words in agony. We did what he asked us to do. We came and sat down in the living room and waited for what would happen next. We could not talk to the gunmen; we were just awaiting their strike.

In the middle of this crisis, a white gentleman in his late 60s, who knew about us, came out from his house nearby to tell the gunmen that we were there as refugees and that the house was ours, but he was told to stay away from the scene. Nevertheless, he persisted until he was allowed to come closer to explain what he knew about us. He told those people, whom we later found out were police officers, that we were refugees from Sudan and that the house was ours, and we were not there as thieves.

A woman who seemed to be in charge called her men to come out of their positions. She then came and knocked at the door, and I opened it for her. She apologized to us, saying that someone from the neighbourhood had called 9-1-1 about a burglary in progress. She promised that from that day on, the police would protect us. The police officers then got into their cars and left. We were relieved. We turned and thanked the neighbour who had come to our rescue.

For the few weeks we were at that home, this neighbour was helpful to us. He invited us over to the house he shared with his son and his daughter with her husband and kids and let us use the phone. Sometimes he would offer to give us a lift to the grocery store for our grocery shopping.

Once the Chesterfield County police officers had left, the blame game started. My roommates started to blame me for the incident.

They thought the problem started because when I rode the bike in the neighbourhood, I might have accidentally passed by the police station. We had seen a huge U.S. flag flying in front of one house in the neighbourhood, and we thought it was a police station. In Kenya, where we lived as refugees, we would only see Kenyan flags at police stations, schools and government institutions. We never saw a Kenyan flag flying over an ordinary citizen's house. My roommates thought it was obvious that the police had followed me after I had passed by them on the bicycle. I could not convince my roommates that there was not any police station in the neighbourhood, and the police did not follow me. The situation became tense as we argued about this, and we were getting ready to fist-fight each other before we convinced each other not to resort to violence. We stayed mad at each other for the next few days.

During these stressful first weeks after our arrival, a man named Jim Einhaus, his wife Lynne Allen and their two sons, Jeff and Colin, got the word from their church and came to visit us. They were members of the Epiphany Catholic Church. They took us out for dinner, and we had our first taste of American food. They also invited us to their home and fed us delicious food, including couscous, a North African dish. They took us out for shopping and bought us warm clothing. They also helped us open our bank accounts and spent countless hours teaching us how to survive in America. They made us part of their family.

Bill, our landlord, and his wife Lisa and daughters also supported us a lot during our first weeks in America. They took us out and introduced us to pizza, and subsequently invited us to their home and fed us delicious food. They introduced us to their extended relatives, and we became part of their wider family.

Having these two American families as our friends, our new life in America felt more promising. We were able to call them in case there was something we could not understand. We trusted them and slowly began to have confidence in ourselves.

After spending three weeks in that house, we moved to an apartment in Henrico County, where we ended up staying for the next five years. About 300-400 Lost Boys and Girls had already arrived and were settled in many different states across the U.S. We gained two more Lost Boys as roommates in December.

Sudanese Community in Richmond, Virginia

After about three weeks, the office of Refugee and Immigration Services found us a two-bedroom apartment at the Nottingham Green Apartment Complex in the Westend of Henrico County in Richmond, Virginia. We were moved to our new apartment the next day. This apartment complex is where the refugee agencies settled most of their newly arrived refugees because of its affordability and proximity to shopping centres and public transportation. I remember our monthly rent during the first six months was $425.

As we were in the car, Marilyn, a volunteer from the refugee office who was helping us move, told us that we would meet many Sudanese in our new place. This sounded great to us, and we were eager to be in a Sudanese community again.

Just after we arrived, a Sudanese family from Nubian Mountains came out to greet us and help unload the truck. We were relieved, though the family was not from our Dinka tribe. In this apartment complex, there were about seven apartments occupied by Sudanese families. Additionally, starting in January 2001, more "Lost Boys and Girls" were coming from Kenya week after week and getting settled in our apartment complex and those that were nearby. And as a result, our Sudanese community was growing almost every day, and we became very happy. Most of these new arrivals were friends from Kakuma Refugee Camp. Even though the Sudanese community in Richmond was not as big as it was in the camp, we at least had a community, a community in which its members looked after each other.

During our first three months, most of us were still not working, and every day or weekend, we would get together, watch TV and talk U.S. and Sudanese politics. It was a good community, and other

Sudanese from different tribes nicknamed our apartment complex *Hila Dinka*, meaning Dinka Village.

I was in a different place with an unusual culture. Making matters worse, the Refugee and Immigration Services, which sponsored and resettled me, would end its support after three months. This was a worrying thing as every refugee coming to America was informed about the agency's end of service just 90 days after arrival. I knew I would be expected to take care of myself after those three months expired.

Spending almost a decade in Kakuma Refugee Camp, where there was nothing but mud huts with tin or palm tree leaf roofs, Sudanese refugees who immigrated to Richmond was not equipped with the necessary skills required to survive in the most advanced country in the world. We didn't know how to shop for food in the supermarket, cross the road, catch a bus to work or cook on a stove. Our adjustment to a new life in the United States would not be easy. We struggled with this uncertainty in Richmond and other cities across Virginia during our first few months in the United States. We began to question if we would really be able to realize our dreams in this unfamiliar, foreboding environment. Luckily, however, as the refugee agencies seemed to be reducing their support, many Americans came to our aid. They came forward as volunteers and became good friends.

When we first moved there, we did not have cable or a VCR in our apartment, and therefore we could only watch movies in our friend's apartment. This was where I first met Jennifer Ernst. She came to visit our friends that afternoon, and she saw me sitting on a sofa. Immediately, she started asking me many questions about where I came from and why I came to the United States. She did not have any idea that many other Sudanese refugees had also come from Kenya. The only Sudanese refugees she knew all came from Egypt. She learned more about us later after she read an article from the Associated Press featuring the three of us, Koul, Peter and I. The article was the first in Richmond to publicize our arrival and what we went through during our painful years of separation from our beloved parents.

I invited Jennifer to our apartment that evening to see where I lived, and while she was there, we asked her to help us get beds, mattresses, and a computer through the church. We did not have good mattresses and beds; we were sleeping on the floor on small mattresses brought to us by the Refugee and Immigration Services. My first bed in America came from St. Bartholomew's Episcopal Church.

This apartment was the place where we had our first interview with Associated Press Writer Masha Herbst. She wrote a very touching article titled "Refugees from Sudan find New Life in Richmond," which came out on the morning of December 31, 2000. We were among the first Lost Boys and Girls who came to the U.S., and the article got a lot of attention. Many hearts were touched. We had never imagined we could become that popular; we thought no journalist would be interested in covering a story of refugees.

After the newspaper story featuring my roommates Peter, Kuol and I, many other newspapers and some local TV stations came to interview us in our apartment. As a result of the publicity, many volunteers came forward to help us understand our new country and its culture. We were invited to Americans' homes for family dinners and to their churches. These volunteers also helped many of us find jobs, learn how to drive, and enrol in English as Second Language (ESL) classes.

Our second meeting with Jennifer, and the first with her husband, Darryl, was when they came to pick up two of the original refugees, Adega and Jook, to go with them to the airport to receive a new refugee, Alor Kuol, en route from Cairo, Egypt. Jennifer asked me if I would go with them, and I agreed. This was the first time for me to see Richmond International Airport since our arrival. We received Alor and brought him to his new apartment. It was a Saturday afternoon. Jennifer asked if I would come to their church on Sunday, and I said, "Sure," but added that the problem would be the means of getting there. "Don't worry," she said, "we will pick you up or ask Adega to bring you." Adega was the only person among the Sudanese refugees in our apartment complex who owned a car. The following morning, I went to St. Bartholomew's Episcopal Church with Adega. The church was small, but the members, who were mostly senior citizens, were great, friendly, and welcoming.

After going to this church for several Sundays, I felt more confident and finally decided to make it my home. After a while, Jennifer and Darryl became my close friends and occasionally invited me and my two roommates, Kuol and Peter, for dinner at their house. A few weeks later, we had two new roommates, Justine Akoon and Garang Marach, who also came from Kakuma Refugee Camp, and Jennifer and Darryl made them their friends too. There were now five roommates in our small, two-bedroom apartment, but we loved it.

As our friendship grew, Jennifer and Darryl helped us understand American culture by taking us to baseball games in downtown Richmond, to American football in different high schools, and to the fireworks on the Fourth of July. They also taught us to know how to shop and cook. Our friendship was making us one family.

Four of us in our apartment were now going to church at St. Bartholomew's, all of us except Peter, who was going to St. Mary's Catholic Church because he was a member of a Catholic Church in Kakuma Refugee Camp. More Lost Boys were still being brought in weekly by the three local agencies, Catholic Charities, Refugee and Immigration Services and the Virginia Council of Churches.

Every Sunday morning, the volunteers from St. Bartholomew's would go around to different apartment complexes and collect the Sudanese refugees for Sunday services. The church's rector, The Rev. Malcolm Turnbull, had a special place in his heart for the Sudanese refugees, and after the church service, he made sure that he greeted his Sudanese parishioners and made them feel at home. There was a lot of support from the church. Donations of all kinds were made available for the refugees, and food banks were stocked with food for the Sudanese families that might not have enough to eat in their apartments.

The church director for outreach and refugees was also working hard to find free dental care for us. Culturally, in the Dinka and Nuer tribes, the bottom teeth are removed from young children as part of initiation and preparation for adulthood. Most of the refugees going to St. Bartholomew's were from the Dinka tribe and were missing their bottom teeth because of this tribal ritual. Jennifer worked hard to find dentists who would volunteer their services to provide false teeth to the Dinka refugees in the Richmond area. I became one of the beneficiaries.

One year after we began attending St. Bartholomew's, the Rev. Malcolm retired. The Rev. Mario Gonzales was named in January 2001 as an interim rector. Now with the Rev. Gonzales heading the church, the Sudanese became more fully integrated into the church. As a result, we received even more help not only from St. Bartholomew's but also from different churches within the Episcopal Diocese of Virginia.

Search for a Job in America

Desperate for my first job in America, I asked Jennifer if she could help me secure a job. It was March 2001, three months after my arrival in America. The refugee agency, Refugee and Immigration Services, had also been trying to find me a job, but they were having a hard time. Some of my roommates and other friends had found jobs. I was the only one in the apartment who wasn't accumulating that valuable and essential American commodity – dollars. All of my roommates were employed and were each bringing home about $240 a week, which made me feel bad about myself. I also wanted to make the precious dollars to help friends left behind in the refugee camp, whom I had promised to help financially after my arrival in the U.S.

Two weeks later, I had a job interview at TMS, a woodworking factory in the West End of Richmond, VA. The Mill Specialist (TMS) was a small family-owned company with fewer than 100 employees, most of whom were immigrants with no prior experience. The starting pay rate was between $7 and $7.50 an hour. Lack of English wasn't a problem. Three of my four roommates, as well as other Sudanese refugees, were employed there.

Jennifer picked me up at 9:30 a.m. I was dressed in my best shirt and tie and waiting eagerly by the door. We headed to TMS and arrived there 15 minutes before the scheduled time. While we waited in the reception area, my heart was beating very fast, but I still had a sense that nothing would prevent me from getting that job. A few minutes before the interviewer's arrival, I was given some forms to fill out. Unlike some refugees, I didn't have any problem with that because English wasn't an obstacle. The interview went smoothly. I got the job, and I was told to begin the following morning at $7.50 an hour for the first three-month probation period, after which a job performance review would determine my pay raise. Despite the low pay rate, I was excited and couldn't wait to start the next day.

After the interview, I was taken for a tour of the company. As the interviewer opened the door leading to the work site, I could hear the noise of the machinery. The air was heavy with dust, smoke and the strange smell of oil. It was too warm inside, and the workers were sweating heavily, already exhausted in their early morning hours. All the employees were wearing goggles, nose masks and earplugs. I was also wearing mine as per the company safety policy. As I looked around, I could see all these strange machines with razor-sharp teeth and blades that looked ready to grab your fingers. I saw one strange machine they called "the belt sander" – it scared me as I watched it slowly consume a long thick wooden door, grinding it to remove its rough parts.

As we proceeded into the factory, we saw a serious, white gentleman standing in a military style and shrieking at one of the employees that his negligence had led to the machine's breakdown. The situation looked very tense, and I was frightened. As we went from department to department, the employees there looked at me with hospitable eyes. They knew that I would be joining their ranks in just a few hours.

After finishing the tour, we returned to the office, turned in our protective gear and headed out to the car. As soon as I sat down in the car, I tried to give fresh thought to the interview and the company in general, but all I could think about was those machines that scared me to death. This was the first time for me to be around all these kinds of moving parts. The closest thing to such a place I had ever seen before was Don Bosco, a Catholic vocational training school in the Kakuma Refugee Camp, but I had never been inside that facility.

In deep thought, I kept quiet for a while, thinking about how I would tell Jennifer that I didn't want the job. Before I could conclude my thought, Jennifer interrupted and asked whether I was excited.

I looked at her and said, "I would rather get another job than that."

She asked, "Why?"

"Because of all those machines and the boss," I replied.

Jennifer then offered her best advice, saying, "I encourage you to take that job for the time being until you get another one."

"Why," I inquired.

She said, "Here in America, you get whatever is available until you find the job you really want."

As a result, she persuaded me to accept the job. We drove for about 15 minutes and stopped at a K-Mart store on Parham Road. Here, Jennifer bought me clothes and steel-toed shoes for work.

The following morning, dressed in my new work clothes and steel-toed shoes, I rode to work with my roommates. Our friend, also a refugee from Sudan, had a car and gave us all a ride. When I arrived at work a little before 7:30 a.m., standing there was a tall white gentleman in his 40s waiting to give me a card with my name on it. He reached out his hand, and I grabbed it in a handshake. He said, "I am Doug; I will be working with you as your supervisor." He took me to the time clock in the break room and showed me what to do with my card. He slid it into the machine, and the card came out with writing in red indicating the time I came into work. He then placed my card in the metal frame with all the cards for other employees. He told me I would clock out for lunch at noon, clock in at 12:30 p.m. after lunch and out again at 5:00 p.m. when everybody would go home. He told me to do that every day except Thursdays when we had a 45-minute lunch break.

Doug told me that I would be his helper. His department built cabinets, doors, and windows. He was a hard-working guy and smoked a pipe. He ate a turkey sandwich daily. During my two years of employment there, I never saw him eating anything other than a turkey sandwich with a cup of coffee. He was very kind to me and was always willing to help me learn carpentry. He also told me about those who had worked under him during his 30-year career there and then branched out to become successful. He even told me stories about his family and his education. Our acquaintance grew, and we became friends.

However, despite being happy on the job, I still had some concerns for my safety. I was afraid of the machines and the possibility of contracting heart disease from dust and the chemicals we used to paint or polish our products. But I needed money.

More than two months into my employment, the owner of the company, Mr Khan, came to my department one afternoon and asked if I could build 130 windows for him. I gave him a concerned look but reluctantly said yes. Mr Khan then explained what he wanted me to do with some demonstrations and then left. I wasn't sure about what to do since it was the first time for me to work independently and did things that I didn't know how to do. To obey my boss, I started working immediately and asked Doug a lot of questions. He helped me with what I wasn't doing right, and within three days, all 130 windows were built. I went to Mr Khan in his office and asked him to come down to see my work. He came and said he could not believe the great work I had accomplished. He then asked me to paint the windows. I did all the painting in less than three days. I reported to him that everything was ready for shipment, and he was amazed. The assignment was a success. My confidence was growing.

Two days later, Mr Khan called me to his office and expressed his appreciation for my work. He also gave me a $1-an-hour pay raise before the end of my three-month probation period. I was the first to get a pay raise, even before some workers who were employed before me. I was later told that at TMS, people don't get pay raises easily. Some people work for years without being given a pay raise. Mr Khan said that I had a good mind and that he wanted me to go to a carpentry school and learn the trade under the company scholarship program. This scholarship program had never been utilized before, and I would be the first. Mr Khan wanted me to take evening classes while I continued working 40 hours a week until I finished college. He also promised me a good job for me after college. "I haven't even been in the U.S. for one year yet," I said. "Whenever you are ready to go to school, I will help you." he insisted.

Working at TMS presented many challenges, including too much heat during the summer and freezing cold in the winter. In the summer, the heat inside could reach up to 100 degrees, and there was no cooling system in the shop, only in the offices. Fans in the shop just circulated the heat and even seemed to make it worse. Then, in the winter, it was always cold inside despite the fact that the heat was on. Doors to the outside would always be left wide open for trucks making deliveries.

Much of the time, regardless of weather conditions, I was outside either doing the roof coating or throwing pieces of wood into a big ugly machine to crush them. I was frequently asked, together with a gentleman from Nigeria named Samuel, to climb to the rooftop and do the roof coating even if the heat felt like it was near the boiling point. Sometimes I just wanted to quit; however, I needed money for rent, and so I was forced to endure such hardships. Sweat would gush down my face and whole body, soak my clothes and then dry up when it wished. From time to time, I would come home with dizziness or an excruciating headache, but I could do nothing to escape because I needed the job. When I complained about it one day, the boss told me I could go home and be in a room with air conditioning or else do the job. I did the job because I didn't want to lose it.

In the winter, I would be sent outside either to crush unwanted pieces of wood in the machine or clear the dusty bag from the chimney. Bags were used to trap dust and direct it into a truck under the chimney that would then transport it to a place of its disposal after it was full. Cleaning these things would cover my whole body in dust, in my nose, ears, everywhere. I was afraid that I would develop a heart or lung condition from that job. Every day, I would complain but would be told that I must do any designated job. The smell of the dust from different kinds of wood made me dizzy and tired. I was afraid of contracting pneumonia because of it being too cold outside. I was told that I must dress warmly daily, but I would still feel the cold even if I wore several layers of clothing. I was also required to wear goggles, a mask, and earplugs, but all these made my hearing, vision and breathing uncomfortable. This caused a conflict with my boss because of safety concerns.

To make matters worse, one afternoon, a supervisor named Owens from the finishing department came to me as I was working outside and told me that I was going to be given one additional assignment. I hoped he was going to give me a new assignment inside, helping him in his department or loading the truck, but my thought was wrong. He said, "Maker, you are going to be cleaning the restroom every Tuesday and Thursday, and you will be given an additional $1 on top of your current hourly pay." "Why me?" I inquired, and he replied, "You have been chosen to do that for the company." This restroom was the only one used by more than 70 employees. Rayray from Vietnam used to do that job, but he had quit because he said he was being bullied by some notorious co-workers who like to pick on people. I said to Owens that I wasn't going to do it. Being a good guy, Owens left without saying any more. I went to the office and asked Mr Khan why he had chosen me among more than 75 workers. He said, "I just want you to do that job. I did it myself when I was young while my father owned this place." In reply, I told him that I wasn't going to do it. He didn't say anything more, and I left. I was ready to quit the job that day.

My objection was not that there was anything wrong with cleaning the bathroom, but it was based on the fact that in Sudan, Arabs, our enemies, used the people of southern Sudan and from other marginalized areas to clean their bathrooms and called them "abit," or slaves. I would not do it because it was so humiliating to me to be assigned a housekeeping job when I was initially hired as a helper in the cabinet department. I knew that I didn't sign up for a housekeeping job at TMS, and if I wanted such a job, I would have applied for it somewhere else. I refused to take it on and was ready for any backlash, but there was none.

Sometimes TMS had the same problems that occur in a prison where inmates are confined together all day. Five members of the cabinet department did most of the bullying. Some employees just voluntarily quit as a result, like little Rayray, who was made mad after dirty water was repeatedly thrown at him while sitting on the toilet seat. His friend and a fellow countryman, Wiw-wi's food, was often frozen solid after being placed in the meat section of the freezer, which meant, most of the time, he would go without eating lunch. Some employees did fight back but ended up being fired.

I was not spared from the bullying. One afternoon as I was busy in the department, trying to meet the deadline for glueing together a sizable number of timbers, which would be turned into doors, one guy from the group came down to my place and took all the clamps I was using to do my job. I asked him why, and he said, "They are mine." I said to him you should have let me finish with them first and then bring them to you. The guy apparently didn't like what I said and punched me in the chest. Standing nearby was a supervisor named Ali from another department. He was from Bosnia and a good guy. He intervened and told me not to hit back but to wait and report the case to a supervisor. When Orlando, one of the supervisors, came, the guy started to threaten me. "Orlando, if you don't take this stupid African boy away from here, I am gonna kick his ass." He was shouting and advancing toward us. He had one of the short clamps in his hand and tried to hit me with it; he missed, and I quickly hit back. My punch landed straight on his nose. His nose and mouth were bleeding. The boss was called in, and I was fired on the spot. I clocked out and went home without saying a word.

I later learnt that the company was in chaos after I had left the building that day. Many faulted the boss for making a decision to fire me without first investigating the cause of the problem. Some claimed that he should have asked the witnesses and learned the facts of the incident before making his decision. Some even claimed that both of us should have been fired. Others took it even further and called it a "racist" decision. As a result, the boss reconsidered his decision. As I opened the door to my apartment, the phone was ringing. It was Mr Khan who asked me if I would return to work. I said, "Yes, but not today." And he said, "it's Ok, see you in the morning." The next morning, I went back to work, and many employees who were one-time victims of bullying welcomed me warmly and called me their hero. Mr Khan came down, pulled me aside and told me that his decision the day before was because he didn't want Albert, the guy I had fought with, to call the police. He added that the police would have been on Albert's side because of the blood from his nose and mouth. He apologized and said he didn't have any ill-intention against me when he made his decision. I accepted his apology and went to work.

Working at TMS for a year now, with all these kinds of experiences, had cultivated my interest in going to school. I revisited my conversation with Mr Khan about sending me to school. One afternoon during my lunch break, I went to Mr Khan's office and told him I wanted to attend J. Sergeant Reynolds Community College. "What are you going to take there?" he asked. "English," I said. He said he would love to help me and discuss the matter with his team in the finance department and see what they could come up with. The following day, he called me to his office and told me that the company was going to pay my tuition while I still worked for them full-time.

The next day I went to J. Sargeant Reynolds Community College for admission. They told me that the first thing I had to do was take English as Second Language (ESL) classes. I was told to return the following day and take an English placement test. I came back, took it and was recommended, based on the test scores, to take Eng. 12 and 13, both writing classes; Eng. 08, oral communication; Eng. 17, a reading class; and Eng. 18, a workshop. Mr Khan paid for one class; St. Bartholomew's Episcopal Church paid for the other class and books. I was excited to be able to go to school and learn so I could have a better job. I was taking evening classes. I would take my schoolbooks, clothes and shoes to work with me. Promptly at 5:00 p.m., I would rush to the bathroom, wash off the dust, change out of my work clothes into clean ones, and head to school for my classes. I would arrive at school 30 minutes early and wait for my class to begin. The class would then run from 6:00 to 9:45 p.m. I would arrive home a little after 10 p.m., find something to eat and then go to bed. The next day, I would get up again at 6:30 a.m. and head to work. I would do this four days a week for my two classes.

My job was a physical one, and I needed to relax but could not do it because of school. Sometimes, I would sleep in class, and my professor would ask me to go to the restroom and wash my face with cool water.

One night when the class had run long, I wanted to rush home and sleep. I came out from the west parking lot, drove to the stop light at Parham Road and waited for the light to turn green so I could turn left. The light turned green, and I made the left turn. As I made the turn, my thoughts were in bed; I was tired and half sleeping. Suddenly I saw a policeman standing in the middle of the road, yelling, "Stop! Stop! Stop!" I quickly slammed on my brakes and came to a full stop. As I looked around, I saw lights on the road and finally realized that it was an accident.

I hadn't had a chance to see the condition of the people involved, but it looked really bad. Two cars collided head-on, and both were totalled. I was shocked to realize that I was about to kill people, including the policeman. As I came to a complete stop, the policeman asked me to drive and turn right onto Lydell Street and wait for him there. He followed me to where I had stopped.

He looked at me through the window with his flashlight shining directly on my face and said, "Have you been drinking, sir?"

"No sir," I replied.

"Have you been taking drugs, sir?" he asked.

"No sir," I responded.

"Why are your eyes red, sir?" he inquired.

"I am tired, sir; I left home this morning at 6:30, went to work until 5:00 p.m. and went to school from 6:00 to 9:45," I explained.

"Let me see your driver's license, please", he requested.

I took out my wallet, pulled out my license and gave it to him. He didn't go back to his car as police would normally do; instead, he looked at it and gave it right back to me. "Sir, you can go now but go home and go straight to bed; your body needs some sleep."

I thanked him for his kindness. I realized later that he based his decision to let me go largely on the fact that he saw my school bag on the passenger seat and on his own understanding as a human being.

Balancing school and work was never easy; nevertheless, my classes were interesting. I was getting what I needed to learn, and I benefitted from being in the class with people from different countries with diverse cultures.

After going through these difficulties for a year, I decided to work part-time and attend school full-time. I had to choose either to quit and find a part-time job somewhere else or convince Mr Khan to let me work part-time even though his company's policy does not allow it. I asked Mr Khan if he would let me work part-time. He agreed. After that, I worked 24 hours three days weekly and brought home around $150. This wasn't enough to pay for my apartment and all my bills, including food, car insurance, gas and other expenses. Still, I tried hard to balance my needs and make good use of what I earned. During this time, three of our roommates had moved, and only two of us were left in the apartment to pay the rent of $500 per month plus bills. Peter was concerned about my decision to work part-time because he thought he would be responsible for paying rent and bills alone. He talked to me occasionally about the prospect of me keeping a full-time job, but I was obstinate. I would tell him just to pay his share of the rent and bills and leave me to take care of mine. For this reason, I had to struggle to make sure that my share of rent and bills were paid on time. I knew very well that things were really going to be hard for me, but I had planned to hold on until I reached my goal.

Jennifer and Darryl were astonished by my struggle and offered to have me move in with them. They designated one room in their house for me and named it "Maker's bedroom", but I didn't accept their offer. I wanted to be independent and learn how to survive on my own in America. After failing to convince me to move in with them, Jennifer suggested that I apply for food stamps so I would be able to use the little money I had for rent and bills. My income would have qualified me for food stamps, but I said I didn't want someone asking me all the time to justify myself. I did not want to survive on the handouts in America as I did in Kakuma.

Now that my work hours were shorter, I had time for my assignments and went to school better-rested and alert. I wanted to hold on to that job until I finished school. But, one afternoon, things changed unexpectedly. My boss came to the department and saw me throw a small piece of wood, less than 12 inches long, into a trash can. He asked me why I threw such a piece of wood away, and I told him there was no use for it since it was so short. I also told him we usually threw away pieces even thicker and longer than that because we couldn't use them. He was angry. He told me that I was fired. "Clock out and go home."

Now I was home with no job. My roommate was the only person in the apartment working, bringing home only enough money for his share of the rent and bills. I had no money saved for unforeseen cases like this because I had not worked long enough to save. Things were getting harder and harder, and the pressure against me was mounting. I needed something soon to help me out of my situation. Without my $150 a week, I could picture myself homeless on the street.

Reluctantly, I decided to go to the unemployment commission and apply for benefits. Within a few days, however, I received a shocking letter in the mail. It said I could not qualify for benefits because I had been fired for insubordination. After reading the letter, I became quite sad, not because I was denied benefits but because the decision was one-sided. I was not consulted about the accusation, and the commissioner accepted it. It was the saddest thing that the commissioner didn't investigate thoroughly before making a decision. Later that evening, I took the letter to Jennifer, who was also troubled by its contents. She told me she would go with me to the unemployment commission and challenge their decision. I said I appreciated her sympathy but that we should not challenge the unemployment commission's decision. I said that if someone had made up this story to distort the facts, it was not worth pursuing, and I was sure I would find another job.

Indeed, within a few weeks, I received a phone call from Beth Shalom Nursing Home to interview for a position in the kitchen. It was exciting news, not because I would love the job but because I would just be able to pay my bills. The kitchen was run by Sodexo, a Richmond food services company contracted to provide well-balanced meals to elderly residents in the nursing home. I was hired in June 2003 as a dietary aide for $7 an hour. My job included helping in food preparation by doing tasks such as cutting onions and making sandwiches, as well as delivering food to units, collecting dishes and washing them, mopping floors and dumping trash in the dumpster after work.

The schedules and hours were good. I would go to work from 3 to 10 p.m. Monday through Friday and anytime on weekends. This schedule allowed me time to go to school in the morning, alert and focused. I worked 31.3 hours a week and made $219.10 before taxes. Overall, the move to this job was a good decision; however, I had some difficulties there, too. I could not get along well with some of the employees. Many of them were less educated and had ghetto attitudes. They tried to bully me when they asked me about kitchen stuff I didn't understand. They would say, "Why don't you understand things — you claim to be a college student?" and then laugh. It was very upsetting, but there was nothing I could do because I needed the job. I tried hard every day to control my nerves for one year until I left for another job.

Walmart, Stores, Inc.

In August 2004, two of my roommates, Sunday and Maker and other Sudanese friends were hired at Walmart Stores as cashiers, cart pushers, stockers, sales associates and loaders in the receiving department. They started at $7-$8 an hour. They were allowed to design their own schedules to balance work and school. For this reason, they liked their managers and were happy with their jobs. They encouraged me to apply for a position there where they thought I could make more money than at Beth Shalom Nursing Home. I applied for a cashier position. To increase my chances of being called for an interview, my friends encouraged me to call the personnel office and follow up on my application. I called, and right then, they asked me to come in at 9:00 a.m. the next day for an interview. I was hired pending the outcome of a drug test. I went straight to the lab. Three days later, I attended orientation. I was given a vest and badge and started work the same day.

Despite standing on my feet most of the time, I loved my job and worked very hard. I made some good friends among the employees, supervisors and managers and was trained on numerous jobs within the store. Still, there were some problems at work. Customers would occasionally give employees a hard time while the management protected the interests of the business and not the employees. For example, in the summer of 2006, a young customer was checking out at one of the express lanes at the Short Pump Walmart one busy weekend evening. She was in a rush and wanted to leave the store quickly. She had a few items in her hand; among them were a box of ice cream and a carton of beer. The line was long and seemed to her to be taking forever. The register operator was a newly hired young African American in his late teens. He was a friendly boy with braided hair and gold teeth. He always had a smile on his face and was loved by co-workers and customers. As the line slowly moved forward, it came to be the turn of the impatient customer. The cashier greeted her by saying, "How are you doing this evening? Have you found everything you have been looking for?" The customer did not reply to the questions. She was angry and just wanted to check out and leave. The cashier didn't say anything more but continued checking out her items until, in the middle of the checkout, there was a prompt from the register to check the customer's ID. The cashier stopped and asked the customer to present her ID as required by law. The customer was infuriated. She picked up the ice cream and threw it at the cashier, hitting him straight in the face. The assistant manager was called in and quickly, without investigation, fired the cashier on the spot.

During my five-year employment with Walmart, I also had my share of difficult customers. One day, a man in his late forties came to Customer Service with a basket full of small pieces of electronic equipment. He pushed his cart toward the counter and handed me a bunch of receipts. I politely said to him, "Sir, can you sort all these items by their receipts and put aside anything you don't have a receipt for?" The man became very confrontational and started cursing at me.

Similarly, on one of the busiest weekend evenings, an old lady came to Customer Service to pay her telephone bill. The bill was past due by three days, and she wanted to pay it that evening. I told the customer I could not help her because the store's policy restricted me from processing past-due bills. She berated me by saying, "This is America; don't you come here and make your own rules. Go back to Africa and make rules over there. Your country does not even have rules."

My years at Walmart introduced me to the degrading treatment of low-wage employees in the United States. I was even more determined to complete my education as a means of finding better employment.

Search for the Family

Months into my new life in the United States, I galvanized my thoughts about finding my family. It had been more than 20 years since we were brutally separated, and my hope for reuniting with them had waned. However, my gut told me to try one more time and hope for the best. For years, I had made many failed attempts to locate them even though I did not have money. But now that I was employed and receiving an income, I thought it would be possible for me to engage someone to travel to the village of Karic in southern Sudan and trace my family. I imagined that by then, people had returned to their devastated villages after the war subsided to reestablish their lives. I also hoped my family would have done the same if they had survived the war.

I had just been employed at TMS and started to receive weekly payments of $250. I reserved this for the search of my family. With money in hand, I had thought of a friend of mine who lived in Nairobi, Kenya but travelled to southern Sudan frequently. She worked for a UN agency, and her job required her to make regular visits to the war-torn region of southern Sudan. I hoped she would take time out of her busy schedule to travel to Karic. Thus, I contacted her and pleaded with her to go to my village the next time she was in the country and search for my family. She agreed and promised to let me know when she was ready to travel.

When she called to inform me of an upcoming trip, I sent her $200 to facilitate her journey to my village. She got very lucky on the first day of her arrival in Rumbek. She was referred to someone who happened to be my uncle, my father's stepbrother. My uncle was the executive chief of Atiaba Payam. Chiefs were and still are very important in Africa and in Sudan in particular. If you needed to find anybody in the village, you would have to look for a village chief. Therefore, my friend was in the right place on her path to find my family. My uncle was very happy when the news was broken to him.

He was excited about the news that I survived the war and was in the U.S. He then led her to my family, and the whole village celebrated the news. There was no telephone communication in the village, so I could be called and informed about the great news. Therefore, I had to wait anxiously for weeks to receive this happy report from her.

Two weeks later, however, I received a phone call from an unfamiliar person. He was my younger brother Akot. Initially, I was sceptical of the caller. Still, a friend who had brought him to Kenya grabbed the phone and told me it was my younger brother Akot and that I should talk to him. I was happy and did not know what to do. I dropped the phone in the middle of our conversation. I celebrated the good news before I could even ask him about the rest of the family. My friend had decided to bring him to Nairobi so we could talk on the phone since there was no telephone communication in the village. My brother came to confirm that I was alive and would take the message back home to the rest of the family.

Initially, I couldn't believe that it was him. He was just a baby when we were separated and now had a deep voice of a young man. Part of the reason I was slow to accept it was him because I knew of Sudanese refugees who had received calls from Kenya from people pretending to be family members. Their purpose was to extort money. I came up with the idea of verifying his identity by asking him about the names of my grandmother, siblings, cows, my childhood name and his, and he answered them all correctly. I burst into tears of joy. My celebration continued throughout the day and night. I bought pizza and beer for my roommates and friends to celebrate with me. Everyone was happy and wished the same could happen for them since they were going through the same ordeals.

I sent my brother money the next day and asked him to purchase some goods in Kenya before returning home. A few months later, Akot returned to Kenya with my other younger brother Juma. I also arranged for my parents to be transported to Kenya so I could talk to them on the phone. Likewise, my sister and other relatives travelled to Uganda, so they also had a chance to talk to me by phone. It was a great moment for the family and me. The first thing they asked was my childhood name, *"ee yin Sabit?"* (Are you Sabit?) and I would respond yes, and they would laugh loudly.

For the next few years, I supported my family financially and paid medical bills for those who were sick. I also sent my brothers and some relatives to school in Kenya and Uganda through support from friends in the U.S. It was remarkable that I was able to trace my family when I had given up my hope of reuniting with them. Some of my friends had given up on finding their families because of many failed attempts in Kakuma Refugee Camp through International Rescue Committee (IRC) letters exchange program.

Now, after knowing that my family had survived the war and were in the village in southern Sudan, my next plan was to travel to the village and be reunited with them. I excitedly prepared for the trip, but it wasn't easy. It took me more than 4 years to finally travel home and reunite with the family.

A Church Adopts the Sudanese Refugees

As the relationship grew between the church and the Sudanese refugees, Jennifer, the director of the church outreach, was inspired to go to Africa to see the places where most of her new friends came from. In the summer of 2002, she joined a mission team from the Diocese of Virginia. The mission team travelled from Richmond to visit the countries of Kenya and Uganda.

In Uganda, the team visited a hospital that was supported by Christ Church Episcopal in Alexandria, Virginia. While in Nairobi, they visited the Church Mission Society (CMS), an organization for British missionaries founded in the late 1970s. This organization was originally established to support the people of southern Sudan but now covered the whole of East Africa.

After these two places, the team proceeded to Kakuma Refugee Camp in north-western Kenya. It was where most of Jennifer's Sudanese friends came from. She wanted to see and experience the place where we had lived for many years. During the team's visit to Kakuma, Jennifer was impressed by how many youths expressed a desire to further their education.

After two weeks in Africa, Jennifer returned to Richmond with a better understanding of the needs and ambitions of the Sudanese refugees living in Kenya and Uganda. She talked to Darryl, and they agreed that they should find a way to provide secondary school scholarships to the students in the Kakuma Refugee Camp.

A scholarship fund was established at St. Bartholomew's Episcopal Church. Jennifer and Darryl donated to three students in Kenya. A friend of Jennifer's was also inspired and sent five orphans and refugees to school in Uganda. A group from Christ Episcopal Church sent a student to school in Kenya. All of these funds were channeled through St. Bartholomew.

While she was at Kakuma Refugee Camp, Jennifer had seen strong faith within the people of southern Sudan. Soon after she got back from the mission trip, she showed me the video of a church service recorded when she was there. She asked if the Sudanese in Richmond would be interested in doing their own church services on some Sundays. The following morning, she called Rev. Gonzales, and he agreed. I talked to my fellow Sudanese friends about the idea, and everybody was excited. In our local Sudanese community, we had strong believers who were brought up in the Anglican Church and became teachers and evangelists in the refugee camp. They had great skills and were qualified enough to lead us in worshipping God in our own Dinka dialect, though none was an ordained minister. Many Sudanese living in Virginia, from as far away as Norfolk, Newport News, Northern Virginia, and Roanoke, began attending our church service monthly. The church was a place where we could socialize. Attending the monthly Sudanese church service at St. Bartholomew's was always a great opportunity.

Meetings were held there most of the time when our church and political leaders visited from Sudan. These included the former vice president of Sudan, Mr Abel Alier, who came in 2002 to brief us on the political situation in Sudan and the then ongoing peace talks between the Sudan People's Liberation Army/Movement and the National Congress Party, the ruling party in Sudan, and Dr Riek Machar Teny who visited us in 2003.

In addition, the Rt. Rev. Bishop Daniel Bul from the Diocese of Renk, who was later consecrated as the Archbishop of the Episcopal Church of South Sudan, visited our church on numerous occasions. In those early years, our church became a centre for activism to raise awareness about Sudan's then distressing and escalating conflict. The church also became a spiritual centre where those who wanted God to hear their prayers could go and ask for blessings.

Soon the small St. Bartholomew's Episcopal Church was becoming overwhelmed with such vast needs. The Ernst family began reaching out to other local churches. I also became part of that effort by mobilizing the Sudanese youth to participate in fundraising events. And as a result, from 2002-04, we were able to raise a lot of money for our ESL classes that were intended to prepare us for GED. Our program was successful because of the publicity given to us by the local media.

Our local Lost Boys and Girls were getting scholarships to community college. Through this effort, the church's account was being flooded with many donations, which overwhelmed the church's volunteer treasurer. The church asked Jennifer to either stop fundraising or find another venue for the Sudanese finance responsibilities. At first, Jennifer was devastated and discouraged. She invited me over to her house and told me about the church's decision.

As we thought about how we should go about keeping our program going, we decided to consult with the former Bishop of the Diocese of Virginia, the Rt. Rev. Francis Campbell Gray, who had been very supportive of the Sudanese community during his tenure as an Assistant Bishop in the Diocese of Virginia. Jennifer contacted him and told him about our urgent need to form an organization. Two days later, we had breakfast together at a coffee shop in Henrico County. We discussed the possibility of forming an organization where we could help those in need. Bishop Gray promised to help find an attorney who would volunteer to help us form a nonprofit organization. Two days later, Jennifer got a phone call from an attorney and an accountant who would prepare some financial documents for the organization.

Within a few months, Hope for Humanity, Inc. was born. Now we were able to operate independently and were, therefore, able to raise more money for our local and international scholarships. We organized a fundraising event through the church, a Walk for Sudan, at which we raised about $20,000. Proceeds from this event were split between the Dioceses of Renk and Rumbek in Sudan. The Renk

Diocese used its money for buying school supplies for its secondary school, while Rumbek Diocese sought to build a new school.

The Lost Boy Finds a Way Home

After years of supporting Sudanese students in boarding schools throughout Kenya and Uganda, the Hope for Humanity members felt that it was time to undertake the construction of a secondary school in the south of Sudan. Of course, I wanted the school to be built close to my village, so my cousins, nieces and nephews and the children in my hometown would have a school close to home. A team from the church planned to make a trip to Sudan to study the logistics of building such a school. They wanted to look at some potential sites and assess the need for themselves. This mission trip in 2005 would prove the opportunity that I was seeking to return to my village and reunite with my family.

My eagerness to return home had been tempered by the reality that I was now a full-time student with no money. I struggled with this and sometimes gave up on the idea. However, Darryl and Jennifer encouraged me to write a letter to the board of Hope for Humanity, Inc. and ask that I be allowed to raise money for my trip to Africa through the organization. I wrote the appeal letter, and my request was overwhelmingly approved.

This approval encouraged me to reach out to friends for help funding my trip. Within a few days, donations started flowing in, and by the end of the month, I had raised more than $4,000. This was enough for all my immunization shots at a travel clinic, air tickets, accommodation, food and other services. Until we left, checks were still being sent in for my trip, for which I was so grateful.

There was still another stumbling block. The U.S. Department of Homeland Security was slow in processing my refugee travel document because so many applications were pending before mine between August and December 2004. Mine was set in December. I waited in despair for two-and-a-half months without any news regarding the processing, except for a letter which acknowledged receipt of my application. It said the processing would probably take about 445 days, which was more than a year.

After waiting for more than two months, my concern grew. In addition to the refugee travel document, I would also need to apply for a visa to Kenya. That would also take time to process. Our departure date was fast approaching, with nothing yet accomplished. We feared that my application might not be approved.

When I finally received my travel document, I discovered some scratches on it that obscured some words and numbers. I hoped that wouldn't cause problems down the road. The Americans on the team who had passports had their visas for Kenya approved the following day. Still, mine, which was a travel document, became another headache. There was no concrete information regarding the steps for visa processing between the Embassy in D.C. and the immigration office in Nairobi. Jennifer had to call the Embassy almost every day, hoping to push for something that would expedite the visa processing, only to be told that the embassy didn't have anything to do with visa approval. Only those in Kenya could make decisions on such a thing. Upon hearing this hopeless response, Jennifer would be frustrated and burst into tears.

Jennifer called a Kenyan woman named Madrine Wawiri, a former church secretary at St. Bartholomew's Episcopal, for help. Madrine knew a woman named Helena at the Kenyan Embassy who could help. She called her the next day, and they spoke for almost an hour. Madrine then called Jennifer and suggested that we try something called "Kitkidoko," meaning giving a little bit of money to Helena at the Embassy so that she would work on speeding up the process. Jennifer felt uncomfortable with this idea as an American, born and raised in a country where it's against the law to bribe; she thought it would be illegal to do and might make things worse.

The irritation grew and grew as the days went by with no news. Jennifer became even more hopeless and discouraged after calling the

Embassy in D.C. and was told that the process would take another 3-8 weeks to complete. There were only three weeks left before our departure. Jennifer started crying soon after hanging up the phone. She called me immediately and told me about it. I calmed her down, saying that God makes miracles and could do something to resolve our situation. "That is true," she said, "only God can make a difference in this case."

We agreed that the Church Mission Society (CMS) in Nairobi could possibly help in this case. Jennifer had already talked to them and asked them to contact the immigration office in Kenya and ask for an expedition of my travel document. These people had already taken numerous trips to the immigration office in Nairobi only to be told that the travel document itself had not even reached the office. According to them, the application and the photocopy of the document had been delayed in transit between the Kenyan Embassy in Washington, D.C., and the Foreign Ministry in Nairobi.

After two days of this terrible and hopeless ordeal, Jennifer received a very encouraging e-mail from one of the CMS officials in Nairobi stating that the travel document had finally reached the immigration office and that the processing would be completed the next day.

With my visa in hand, memories of home flooded my mind. I started dreaming of home again –my family and friends and visiting my childhood places such as Rumbek town, Akot and Karic. My heart and soul had already gone home. My body was the only thing that was still in Virginia. Every day, I felt like I was sitting by the fire with friends and relatives, telling stories. Sudan was nearer than ever before!

Shopping Spree for Gifts at Walmart

After receiving the visa approval to Kenya, word got out that our travel to Sudan through Nairobi was imminent. E-mails for gifts from the U.S. flowed in day and night from students in Nairobi and from family and friends in Sudan. We thought that it was important to consider all requests for gifts and try to bring the requested items to Nairobi and Sudan; however, this became another headache for Jennifer and me.

We began by shopping for shoes, but it was very hard because most of our students didn't know their shoe sizes. They would send us e-mails saying they needed a pair of sports shoes in size 44 or 46 while the actual size could be smaller or larger. Many of them had long feet for which we could not find the right sizes, and we bought and later returned items when we would receive other e-mails requesting different sizes. Shopping for American jeans, as they called them, was also tough because of the problem of sizes. Consequently, the shopping we thought would take one day took us many days. Finally, we bought shoes for 13 students and friends.

We knew that the people in Sudan were in greater need than those in Nairobi; however, we didn't have any clue about their sizes of shoes or clothes they wore. We decided to buy clothes and shoes of various sizes for them, knowing they might use them whether the sizes were exact because they were in such great need.

I asked two Sudanese women in my neighbourhood to help me shop for gifts. We went to Walmart because of its low prices, but also, it was my workplace where I could get a discount of 10% off each item. Akol Awur, Amok Maper and I went to Walmart at around 8:00 a.m., and the shopping took us almost the whole day. It took the three of us a long time to finally agree on clothes to buy, as the two women were very selective. They loved to buy things that looked beautiful and attractive.

After the shopping, I dropped the women off at their apartment. I went straight to Jennifer's house, where we were organizing things for our journey. Jennifer and Darryl were surprised to see how many clothes I had bought. Everywhere in the living room was a pile of clothes as we were trying to sort them out. We had to put all the clothes and shoes designated to one person together in one small shopping plastic bag and then tag it. This process took us days to complete, and we still had to find or buy more bags to carry them to Africa. Two big bags packed with shoes and one other with clothes were going to be left in Nairobi for our students, while another four bags packed with clothes and shoes were going to Sudan. We had to be careful sorting out what was for whom and where it was going. Our plan was that since we were a team of seven people, these extra bags of gifts would be divided into seven so that everyone in the team would include one in the allowed baggage limit. The seven bags were full, and there were still gifts left. No one had any room left.

That evening the whole team came together right before we left and decided to repack the gifts, fitting into our bags whatever we thought was important to take with us and leaving behind what was less important. The work to sort out what should remain behind was tough. Jennifer and I worked on sorting these things until midnight, returning the extras to Walmart, where we got $190 back. The money later helped us at Wilson Airport in Nairobi to pay for more than 20 kilos of our extra weight.

Meeting with our Students in Nairobi, Kenya

After boarding the plane at Dulles International Airport outside Washington D.C., we set off across the Atlantic Ocean and over Europe into East Africa. We arrived in Nairobi on June 2, 2005, at Jomo Kenyatta International Airport. We were processed through security, reclaimed our bags and went to a waiting area to wait for someone from Mayfield Guest House to come and pick us up.

While at the airport, Darryl was trying to make a phone call to the U.S. and let our contact person, his sister Jane, know that the team had arrived safely in Nairobi. She would then send an e-mail to all our friends and family members. However, the call could not go through because Darryl did not know the right international code to use.

While this was going on, there was something else bothering me. As someone who had lived in Kenya for many years, I realized that people were trying to pickpocket Darryl. People immediately surrounded him as he was trying to ask how and where to make a phone call, and every one of them was trying to offer help. I stayed behind Darryl to keep watch. I encouraged him to wait for the bus from Mayfield Guest House and call from there.

The Mayfield driver finally arrived and led us to his bus to load our bags. While we loaded our bags into the bus, several young people were massing around in the hope of pickpocketing us or stealing our bags. Still, now the whole team was very aware and protective of each other.

At Mayfield Guest House, I was anxious to call my brother in Nairobi but did not have the correct number. Instead, I called my friend Gideon, one of our sponsored students who lived near him and told him we had arrived. He gave me my brother's number, but it was not going through. One of my cousins, also one of our students, Peter Mangar, picked up the phone and told me that my brother was spending the night with some friends at their house. I asked him to let my brother and the rest of my friends and relatives know that we had arrived at the guest house.

After breakfast, we went to the Church Mission Society (CMS) office for a meeting. This organization played a crucial role in receiving and administering funds from Hope for Humanity for students going to schools in Kenya and Uganda. As president of Hope for Humanity, Jennifer presented an official framed 'thank you' letter to Sila Matu, who worked closely with her and the students. Sila said CMS was pleased to continue working with Hope for Humanity and that anything that CMS could do to rebuild southern Sudan was crucial to his organization.

Jennifer introduced the team and explained her mission. She asked what Hope for Humanity could do to improve the scholarship program. Sila explained the need for monthly allowances or pocket money, transport, private tutoring during holidays, basic medical care, and better schools that understand the situation of foreign students and the importance of studying English as a learned language so they could cope well in their classes.

We returned to Mayfield Guest House at 3:00 p.m., the time we had promised to meet with our students, including my brother. I had not seen my brother since I was nine years old. A group of people started to arrive, mainly to see me with my visitors. Some were close relatives and friends with whom I had been in the refugee camp five years earlier. A few minutes later came a teacher of my first years of primary and church education, whom Jennifer had been sending to a theological college in Kenya. It was a great moment for my friends and me, and there were a lot of hugs, cheers and joy, even though I could not recognize many of them. Groups came one after the other. It was incredible to be back with everybody.

An hour later, my younger brother Juma arrived. As he approached the gate, he ran, yelling "Sabit! Sabit!" my childhood name. Even though I had pictures of him, they were not enough to recognize him. I realized only when he called me by my childhood name, this was my brother. I started running to him. "Jima! Jima!" I held him tightly, tears in my eyes. He was only two years old the last time I saw him.

This also was a moment of joy for Jennifer and Darryl to be with their students whom they had been sending to school without knowing them properly. They were greeting each other excitedly and asking each other for names. Many more people kept coming, and the Mayfield compound became filled with a large crowd of people. It was overwhelming, and other guests at Mayfield were surprised to see so many people coming in. After all this attention for me and my team, I felt honoured to have this kind of love from my people. I felt welcomed and was grateful to be back with my family. It was a moment I will never ever forget.

After socializing with the members of the Sudanese community in Nairobi, the students organized a meeting as a way of saying "thank you" to their American sponsors, to me as the contact person for the program, and especially to Jennifer and Darryl, who spearheaded this vital program. It was planned so that each student could at least have a chance to stand up and express his gratitude for the scholarship to attend school in Kenya. One student after another expressed the importance of their education to the people in Sudan. Following the speakers, Jennifer stood up and said, "I have seen the need for education from all of you. All of you will go to school." She passed around a notebook for everyone who didn't have sponsors to write in their names for future sponsorship from the U.S. The group erupted in applause.

Flying to Rumbek, Sudan

On June 4, 2005, and after the joyous night spent at Mayfield Guest House with my younger brother, Juma, relatives and friends, the team boarded a small, 12-passenger jet bound for Rumbek, my hometown. I was on my way to see my family. As we passed over the mountains of Nukuru and Kitali, memories of Kakuma Refugee Camp began to disturb my thoughts of Rumbek. It was Kakuma where I had spent 8 lonely years; destitute, worried and always sick, tired and very poor. It was where I never had a choice but to always wait for someone else to make decisions about my life. Because of this, my excitement shifted from happiness to anxiety. In my thoughts, despite being on the plane, I felt like I was back again in Kakuma Refugee Camp, which I never wanted to visit again.

This continued over the highlands of Lokichogio, Nerus, Ngatinga, and Kapoeta, where I really felt the intensity of the civil war in Sudan. This range of highlands was where the consequences of war were deeply felt by many Southern Sudanese. In 1992, government troops from northern Sudan attacked the town of Kapoeta. Many lives were lost, and many survivors became the first refugees at the Kakuma Refugee Camp. Forced to walk for days to cross the border to Kenya without enough food or water, the tired group, afraid and with blistered feet, arrived at the Kenyan border town of Lockichoggio, where they came to face further challenges of water and food shortages, as the United Nations Refugee Agency UNHCR was not prepared for the arrival of such a large group of people.

Flying over this unforgettable death trail and its horrifying memories put me back at the actual scene. These negative thoughts were scrambling in my mind. I realized I was suffering from symptoms of PTSD. As we crossed the Nile River, I recalled another terrible experience in which unarmed and venerable civilians, including my uncle, were killed when Sudanese warplanes dropped bombs directly on us.

Nevertheless, I turned my thoughts to happy memories. I could still sense the fresh smell of a cattle camp, the beautiful sound of cows, the traditional singing of my Dinka people. I could also see all kinds of people sitting in the shades of big and beautiful trees during the day's bright sun. I could hear the sound of small children crying for their grandmothers to feed them more milk. I saw the beautiful green bank of the Nile and felt the cool breeze it splashed out to cool down the hot temperatures in sight of its blue tributaries. These visions became the greatest and most important part of my healing meditation. As we were passing over Yirol and Ruap-apak, I could sense my former cattle camps of Dourpuot, Gadieng, Thielieng, and others. It is where I really enjoyed my childhood.

In the next few minutes, we would pass over Aluakluak, a small town where my mom was born and raised, and also the nearby village of Agany, a place where my grandma still dwells. I could imagine sitting under the shade, near grandma, and surrounded by three aunts with their children. I was sitting under a huge mango tree, inhaling cold fresh air, playing and moulding clay cows out of dirt from termite mounds with my young cousins and friends. I could feel lying on my back on a mat made out of animal skin, sharing and listening to tales about animals people believed used to talk like humans. The short stories from animals such as foxes, hyenas, rabbits, lions, and elephants were very funny, and children liked to hear them. There was one thing about these stories, though. They were never told in the daytime because there was a superstition that people would get lost if they told stories during the day.

In a few minutes, we would be going over Akot town, the place of my childhood where I had unforgettable times with my childhood friends and a pet monkey I named Koko, with whom I shared everything, including food. He helped me fight the notorious boys in the village and climbed the mango trees, and brought me fresh mangos. I would cry out for help if someone tried to take Koko away or abuse him when he snatched bread at a nearby bakery. These memories instantly came back to me after many years of not thinking about them.

Memories about my favourite places for goat and cow herding in the village of Karic, where I lived and went to pre-school in the early 1980s, came back to my mind. More memories of children playing and dancing at night under bright moonlight, the clan elders and the community leaders gathered under trees for communal ceremonies and to settle disputes, the women's groups of all ages. The youths with shields and clubs dancing and celebrating the final release of a bride to her new house were the memories that served as catalysts to my rising excitement as we approached Rumbek. I could also feel myself fishing and dipping in the Bahr el Naam River, the lovely place I spent most of my weekends in September and the whole summer when the school was closed.

In the next few moments, our pilot adjusted the gears, and I felt the plane descend for landing. I could see through the small window some features of my childhood culture – the beautiful huts, tukuls, trees of all kinds and familiar animals. Here I felt the exhilaration of my homecoming and the realization that my long-awaited dream was now becoming a reality.

As the plane was preparing to land, some of the team members, Eric, Darryl and Alberta, adjusted their cameras to take pictures of a dirt airstrip as the plane approached for its final touchdown. In less than a minute, the plane finally landed, blowing dust into the air in spite of the rain in the town a few hours before. The pilot got big applause from the passengers for landing the plane safely in such a tiny airfield with cows and goats grazing on one side of the runway and construction workers on the other.

Rumbek, Sudan

On the ground, the excitement of being back in the town of my birth and a place I had not visited for many years could hardly be contained. The rest of my team alighted the aeroplane first to set up their cameras to capture my first steps back to my homeland. I got out last, and there, standing and waiting for me at the steps of the aeroplane, was my younger brother, Akot, who jumped immediately to catch, hold and hug me before I even put both of my feet on the ground. We could not let each other go for quite a while. My uncles, Chiefs Mangar and Det, cousins and other friends also came to find me. It was an unforgettable grand ceremony, though I could not recognize everybody waiting for me at Rumbek Airport.

There was also a group of about 50 people from the church led by the Assistant Bishop of Rumbek, Joseph Maker Atot. The crowd of church people had been waiting at the airport for many hours since morning, singing and beating druMs. Our team had travelled to Rumbek at a time when no one from the West would visit southern Sudan because of the ongoing war. The Comprehensive Peace Agreement (CPA) had only been in place for 5 months. Our arrival made it seem real. They had been isolated by 21 years of civil war and thought they were forgotten by the rest of the world.

After this great salutation, we quickly went through a very straightforward security check, and then our bags were loaded into a Land Cruiser vehicle. We got in and drove on a bumpy and unpaved road through a barren town with old walls riddled with bullets. In this town, there was no communication system or good markets, no running water, and no health system or good schools. Things were horrible for the people of Rumbek. I saw that the living conditions were miserable.

After a few minutes, we arrived at St. Barnabas Cathedral Church of Rumbek, under a gigantic fig tree in the middle of town. There was a wonderful reception for us. A lot of people, including some parishioners from the nearby churches, came to join the group that had received us at the airstrip and followed us to the church for a special welcoming. Bishop Joseph Maker led the prayer, and then each of us from the team was asked to introduce him or herself in front of the congregation. We could see the anguish of the people, many of whom looked weak and thin, either because of a lack of food or being sick. Some people in the church were half-dressed or had dirty and torn clothes on them. Most people were barefooted. You could clearly see the destruction of war in people and around town. I could not even recognize where I was.

The intensity of the 21-year-long civil war was visible here because only a few things were left standing. The only things left were small trees, grass, enemy tanks, and the new tukuls that were built when the enemy evacuated the town and people returned to rebuild their lives. I realized that the northern troops had destroyed the large trees for better visibility during the rebels' attack on the town.

The reception ended in about half an hour, and then we were ready to go to a hotel. However, there was no car for our ride, and it was too far to walk, so we seemed to be stuck in stinging heat and humidity. We were also tired and hungry because we had left for the airport before breakfast was ready. My brother and cousins were out working hard to find a ride for us. Eventually, they were able to borrow a pickup truck from one of the NGO personnel, and they brought it to the church. The small truck had two doors in front and an open one behind. Since there was not enough space inside to accommodate all of us, Paul, Darryl, and I sat in the back of the truck.

As we set off, the rain that had been building up in the clouds and causing a lot of heat started falling. No one among us had anticipated it so that we might have our umbrellas with us. The rain continued until we arrived at the Bros Hotel, where we would stay.

The rain upon our arrival in town did not seem to strike the rest of the team members the way it struck me. People may believe that the rain coincidentally met our arrival, but for me, as a Dinka steeped in that culture's beliefs and myths, it was a blessing my homecoming was marked with rain. In Dinka culture, people believe that when someone comes home for the first time in many years and the homecoming is blessed with rains, then that person is a blessed person. So, after everything I had been through to get home, the rain welcomed me.

Now we were at the hotel having lunch and relaxing, while many of my relatives came to visit me. Some walked or rode bicycles from villages as far away as 36 miles. Some came from within the town or were students living in dormitories at Rumbek Senior Secondary School. I recognized some of them but not others because it had been so long, and many were young when I left home. Among those whom I instantly recognized were Marel Muka, my uncle from the village of Karic; Athian Manyiel from Adol Primary School; and two of my childhood friends, Mapet Mabor and Majok Mading.

I spent the rest of that evening with so many people coming and going from the villages and town. As I walked through the town, people surrounded me, many I did not know. Apparently, I had become famous as the first lost boy to return home to them.

My cousins joined us. They asked me about my life in the U.S. and what I was doing for my education. We walked up to Freedom Square, then returned to Bros Hotel to prepare for a meeting over dinner with the three bishops of Rumbek.

While in Rumbek, I realized that a lot of things had changed in my absence, but some of the things remained the same. These included the beautiful mooing of cows, the barking of dogs, the braying of donkeys and the laughter of people throughout the night. The morning breezes with cold air enhanced by the singing of all kinds of different birds, cock crows and the gentle hospitality of the people had remained the same over the years despite the destructive conflict in Sudan.

On the morning of June 5, 2005, we wanted to attend the biggest Sunday service under the fig tree at St. Barnabas Cathedral Church of Rumbek. We were told the services would begin exactly at 9:00 a.m. local time. We were told to be ready for church a little after 8:00 a.m. and that a driver would pick us up from the hotel. But the driver didn't show up. We waited until it was almost 9:00 a.m. with no word either from one of the bishops or the driver himself. With the time for the service approaching, we began to be worried about the delay, particularly Rev. Johnson, who was scheduled to give his sermon during church service. It created an uncomfortable mood for all of us because we came from a country where everything runs on time. We were feeling guilty, imagining that someone would take it as being our fault. We waited, waited and waited, but there was no sign of the vehicle promised. Eventually, my uncle, Manyang Makuac asked the manager of Bros Hotel to take us. As it turned out, we were among the first to arrive. The rest of the people filtered in later after we had been there for half an hour.

I know in the West, punctuality is highly regarded, but in Sudan, time is left up to the individual. We could see this attitude in the three bishops throughout the week when they didn't struggle or feel pressured like we did to watch the clock. They knew that the church service wasn't going to start as scheduled. People lived far away. Some walked an hour and a half to get there. Some might be gardeners and might need to work their gardens early in the morning, then walk some distance to fetch water for a shower before walking miles to church for Sunday services.

One by one, people began to arrive, and soon the church became crowded. The church service was led by Assistant Bishop Joseph Maker. Rev. Johnson then gave a powerful sermon to the congregation. It was a wonderful service; Rev. Johnson was preaching in English and being translated into Dinka by Assistant Bishop Dhieu from Akot Diocese. Every word Rev. Johnson said was then followed by great applause from the more than 800 worshippers. His words were very encouraging to the people, giving them a sense of understanding that there are still a lot of people in different parts of the world who are compassionate about the suffering of the people in Sudan. The service ran for three hours, and no one seemed to be wearied by it.

Back at the hotel, we had our lunch and tried to get some rest before going back to church for a meeting that evening; however, we did not manage to rest because many people were still visiting us. This had a great impact on us during the next few days due to the fact that we were exhausted and suffering from the heat of up to 90 Degrees Fahrenheit with 70 per cent humidity.

The State of Education in Southern Sudan

The next day would be our busiest. Our driver, Maben, brought the three bishops to us. The mission team and the bishops got in the Land Cruiser and headed to Rumbek Senior Secondary School. Our aim of visiting was to find out the needs and difficulties facing the school, including how much room the school had, the number of students currently enrolled, and how many could not get in because of a lack of classrooms and accommodations.

Our first visit was to Rumbek One Primary School, an Episcopal mission school that hosts classes ranging from pre-school to primary three, under a giant fig tree. The school lacked teaching materials, proper seating for students and payment for teachers. The students were committed to attending school despite empty stomachs or long walks to the school. We asked some of the teachers why they were doing what they were doing instead of finding jobs in which they might be paid. Their response was that southern Sudan had been neglected for decades without education by the government in Khartoum and needed schooling for the new generation. So, giving the children the little knowledge they had would prepare them for better education during peacetime.

"We cannot wait for peace to come when there will be payment for teachers and then start teaching our children, while our enemy in the north is offering education for its kids and fighting us at the same time. We have to teach our children so that if peace comes, our kids and theirs will be on the same level," said the head teacher at Rumbek One.

Here at school, we saw an older woman sitting in the class with the third graders. She looked to be in her mid-sixties. One of the members of our mission team was a reporter named Alberta Lindsey. When Alberta asked her why she was sitting in the class with kids, she said she was in the class because she wanted to learn and become smart like an American woman. This was a touching answer and a reminder of how the majority of Southern Sudanese who missed out on education during their youth were regretful of their missed opportunity and hungry for education even in old age. This became even clearer when we were going to villages; we were received by hundreds of school kids. There was usually a school within walking distance, unlike in the old days when schools were only built in the major cities and towns of the south but none in the villages. There were now more than 100 primary schools in Rumbek alone and one secondary school compared to five or six during the 1970s and before the war.

After Rumbek One Primary School, we proceeded to Rumbek Girls Primary School. This school was built in the late 1970s, but most of it was destroyed during the war. Only a small portion of it was being used now to accommodate several hundred day-schoolers under UNICEF's support. The classes ranged from pre-school to primary seven. We were impressed and appreciative of the fact that parents had allowed their daughters to go to school and learn instead of keeping them at home as a source of bride wealth to their families. In the old days, girls were not considered important people who could be leaders in the country. They were considered inferior and most valuable as a source of bride wealth. They were expected to remain at home to do household chores and be mothers, while boys were given a chance to go to school. We could see the high interest of women in the south for education through those we visited at school. We looked into their exercise books and found that most of them were doing very well.

In every class we visited at Rumbek Girls' Primary School, students rose to sing songs of welcome, and we could see the happiness on their faces because of our visit. We later saw many other girls' schools in the villages, which was one of the greatest achievements our community ever made.

We left Rumbek Girls' Primary School and headed to Rumbek Senior Secondary, where we were received by the headmaster

Abraham Dut Makoi. He introduced his staff and then began by telling us the history of the creation of Rumbek Senior Secondary School and how it was reopened after Rumbek town fell into the hands of the SPLA in 1997. The secondary school was built in 1948 by the British when Sudan was one of its colonies. It was built not only for the Rumbek community but also to include all the Southern Sudanese. This secondary school happened to be established in Rumbek because the governor of Rumbek won a competition among governors when he wrote an essay explaining why he wanted a secondary school for the whole of southern Sudan built in his area. He made some critical points, among them that Rumbek was the centre of all three regions of southern Sudan, namely, Bahr El Ghazal, which included Rumbek, Upper Nile and Equatoria. He claimed that if people started journeying at the same time to Rumbek, they would arrive exactly at the same time. He won the competition.

The school was built big enough to accommodate over 2,000 students from the three regions of southern Sudan. The same number was admitted each year until 1983 when the second civil war broke out, and the town was taken over by the military from the north.

This school was considered a leader in education, and admission was very competitive. Consequently, students from all over southern Sudan had to work hard during their final year in intermediate school and score certain grades to be accepted. Most of the leaders of southern Sudan between the 1960s-1983 had been students at this school. The school was shut down from 1983 to 1998 due to the war. It reopened in 1998 with support from USAID, which paid for the renovation of some buildings. But not all of its 48 buildings were remodelled, and the number of students admitted dropped from more than 2,000 to 725 because of lack of space. The area has over 1.5 million school children, and most of the children were being turned away because of a lack of rooms and accommodations. As a consequence, graduates of primary schools were forced to either go back to cattle camps where their parents lived or just sit at home hopelessly.

At the meeting, we were also told that among the current number of students enrolled in school, 300 came from Western Bahr El Ghazal alone, while 425 were from other regions and local communities. Among the staff meeting with us was a brother, Mike, from New York. He worked for the Catholic Diocese of Rumbek as a school administrator and chemistry teacher. His diocese sponsored and ran the school, and because of this, he really understood the needs of his school. He told us that there were many students wanting to attend school, but due to the lack of rooms, many were turned away, which he said was sad. "We teach some of the students who could not get a room during the day under trees in the evening," said Mike. We repeatedly heard from the staff that building another school somewhere in Rumbek would help a number of unadmitted students to resume their studies.

After the meeting, Brother Mike and some of his colleagues took us to visit some classes, the dormitories and the dining room. We could see the condition of the school, lack of good benches in the classrooms, no electricity or running water, and not enough teaching materials. As we were taken to a kitchen, we saw women preparing lunch for students. This could be their only meal for the day.

We found that each dorm room accommodates more than 10 students in uncomfortable conditions. Most of the dormitory buildings had walls only without their roofs on because the iron sheets were taken off the walls and used to cover military trenches. We could see most of the walls riddled with bullets or smashed off with mortars. There were also the remains of rusted military tanks and other vehicles directly on the school grounds. We walked pass a deep trench that had been used by the military commander in Rumbek.

Our idea for building another school was proven as something urgently needed by the entire community of Rumbek and the surrounding areas after our visit to Rumbek Senior Secondary School. We also now had a good idea of what we wanted our school to look like.

While touring the school, we also saw the condition of the local people. One woman approached us carrying in her arms a very sick, weak and crippled baby. She asked Jennifer if she could pray for her child. She probably approached Jennifer because she thought she might be a pastor. And to her, prayer from a pastor would be enough to cure her child because it brought her relief.

There was only Rumbek Hospital in the town, run by an international NGO with limited medical supplies and rooms to accommodate the local population. I have seen this on my own when I visited my uncle, who was very sick with stomach and heart disease. He was discharged from the hospital while still very ill and could not walk or feed himself. He suffered at home under the care of his old mother without any medicines. He passed away two days after our return to the U.S. from our trip.

The situation people were going through was very tough, many people looked sick and weak, and there was nowhere for them to get treated. No money for them to even seek medical care in neighbouring countries such as Kenya and Uganda. People just endure their ailments like wild animals.

After the tour of the school, we went straight to the county commissioner's office, hoping to meet the commissioner himself, but he wasn't there. His deputy, Makur Meen, was waiting for us in his office. There was no air conditioning or fan, and the room was very hot. Sitting in front of him was an imprinted wooden shoebill, the county's symbol, and a big old ring binder accounting book from the year 2004. The Bishop of Rumbek Diocese Alapayo introduced the team and our mission. Mr Makur told us the story of Rumbek, from the past to the present and why it had become a great place for many people to live. He also told us a little about their mission as the county authorities and what they could do to help.

He explained that for someone to build something for the public and not for his or her own private business, free land is guaranteed.

Upon hearing this, Rev. Johnson asked him to repeat his words, and he said it again. Rev. Johnson then asked everyone in the team to write that statement down. The Acting Commissioner pledged his support. Because it was hot in the office without proper ventilation, the meeting was wrapped up in less than 30 minutes, and we walked away with the impression that the political and community leaders in Rumbek were supportive of our project.

We went back to Bros Hotel for lunch and prepared for a 4:30 meeting with the three bishops and their aides.

We continued the discussion of the pending projects. Instead of going back to the hotel, we went to my cousin Moses Muorwel's house, where he and my little brother Akot were planning a welcoming party for us. We didn't know that there would be a great party; we thought that we were simply visiting the home. When we arrived, we saw many people, mostly relatives and friends, some of whom had travelled from far villages to attend this event. It was amazing for everybody in the team to witness such a warm welcome.

Soon, however, it was getting dark and to make matters worse, there was no light because there was no electricity or power supplied by a generator. That pressured the women who were working hard to prepare the goat's meat, bread and *asida* to hurry before the sun set. The food was brought, and we ate with the aid of crescent lamps that were placed on the table. It was great hospitality. The food, which included cold drinks, was enough for the guests and everybody who commuted from the villages to attend the event in Rumbek town. Rev. Johnson called this "self-sacrifice" by the family, who had next to nothing yet made such an effort to host a party for us.

After our brief visit to the schools, we headed toward the villages the next day. Travelling on a dusty road worried us because of landmines that might have been set there during the war. It was very hot in the over-crowded Land Cruiser with no air conditioning. We were on the road leading to my village, where I would soon meet my family. I was now only hours and miles away.

We arrived at the Bahr el Naam River. To cross this river, we had to drive on a very small and narrow traditional road where we were scared of possible landmines or the Land Cruiser flipping over on the road. We were thankful for our skilled driver on such a terrible road. Along the way, he showed us the remains of some of the cars that had been blown up by landmines and where a heavy truck coming from Uganda had capsized, killing my childhood friend Marial and injuring others, including my cousin Mangar. There was a point where the driver left the main road completely and drove on a new path created as a safety precaution. Despite the fact the war was over, southern Sudan was still riddled with active landmines.

Because of the poor road, the distance that would usually be covered in under an hour took twice as long. It was a tiresome journey.

It was getting dark, and we wanted to meet the Rumbek East County Commissioner in his office. Bishop Alapayo realized that the office might have closed, and the solution would be to catch up with him in his house. The driver took a turn and headed straight to the commissioner's house. He was home. He welcomed us, and the bishop began to introduce the team to him and explain our mission. He was very thankful for our mission with education and committed to supporting the construction of the school. This commissioner was my relative, and I had been with him and his family for many years in Kakuma Refugee Camp in north-western Kenya.

Money Talks in Kenya

After a week in Rumbek, southern Sudan, we boarded a 12-passenger plane back to Nairobi, Kenya, the first stop on our way back to the United States. Our travelling in the villages in southern Sudan had exhausted us, and we were keen to arrive at Mayfield Guest House, where we could relax and sleep before the long journey the following day to the United States.

When we arrived at Wilson Airport in Nairobi, things started to spiral out of control. The immigration officer in charge at the airport took all our passports and my Travel Document, as is the usual security routine at any airport. Then, to our surprise, he returned only two passports of the seven documents to their owners. Of our team, only Eric and Tracy got their passports back. The rest of us were told that our visas had expired, and, as a result, we were in Kenya illegally.

This sounded alarming to us! In Kenya, a mistake like this could cause someone a huge amount of money. It clicked immediately in my mind that the only solution to get us out of this trouble would be to give the officer "kidkidodo" a bribe to gain his cooperation. As we stood there, exhausted and worried about what would happen to us, Rev. Johnson asked whether we could be granted transit visas. But the short, limping man, who appeared to be in his mid-40s, replied, "Your visas expired the day you left for Rumbek, Sudan because you didn't have multiple visa stamps on your passports." We found out later that anyone who wishes to travel in multiple eastern African countries must acquire multiple visas. The Kenyan Embassy in Washington D.C. had automatically granted Tracy and Eric their multiple visas, although they had not been aware they were any different than the rest.

Again and again, the team members asked the officer to find a way to grant us transit visas since we were just there for one day, but he wasn't willing to help us for reasons he was not stating. The officer would not allow us to buy our visas at the port of entry as allowed by Kenyan immigration law. He stuck with his words and would not entertain our request and repeatedly said that everybody's visa had expired and that we were in the country illegally.

This argument went on for hours, and it became even more irritating to the whole team when he stopped even listening to us – but as someone who had lived in Kenya before, I knew very well what he wanted. He wanted "kidkidoko." He knew that the four members of the team who held U.S. passports could buy their transit visas there for just $10 or $20, but he didn't want us to know that. On the other hand, I knew that my case would be different because I was holding a U.S. refugee travelling document, and that might have some issues with the law of Kenya.

We were tired and hungry, and we just wanted to rush to the guest house to rest and eat, but the airport immigration officer did not change his mind.

For hours we were there, he kept repeating the same thing: "Your visas have expired, and you are in this country illegally. You are in violation of Kenyan law." However, Rev. Johnson stood bravely and exchanged tough words with him the whole time we were there.

Tiring of this argument, the officer went into the small room behind his office for a few minutes, came back and said, "I got two news for you, the bad news and the good news."

"Tell us the bad news first," said Rev. Johnson.

"The boss said, for those of you who have passports, you will be granted transit visas, and the one with the Travel Document will not spend the night here in Kenya," he said.

"Why is he being treated differently from us?" Rev. Johnson asked.

"Because he doesn't have a passport, and the government does not allow us to give transit visas to those who are travelling on travel documents," the officer responded.

"Where are you going to deport him to?" Rev. Johnson inquired.

"The country of his residency," the officer replied.

"We were leaving for the United States tomorrow evening anyway, and therefore, there is no need for us to apply for transit visas, so we can all go to the airport together, and we leave tonight," Rev. Johnson said. "The officer should bring a car big enough to accommodate all the seven of us," Rev. Johnson continued.

After hearing this, the officer seemed to be uncomfortable and ceased to speak for a while. He ran back to the small room, then came out and said, "There is good news. You will all be granted transit visas, which will cost each of you $20." We all said, "Yes," and he gave us transit forms, and we filled them out and paid the fees. After three more hours, we were issued transit visas. We then went to Mayfield Guest House, where we stayed until we left for the United States the following evening.

This incident was not new to me. In 2000, before I went to the United States, I was travelling from Kakuma Refugee Camp to Nairobi with eight other people. We were all travelling on one travel document issued by Sudan Relief and Rehabilitation Association (SRRA) in Lokichogio, Kenya.

The travel document was legal and recognized by the Kenyan government, but with widespread corruption in the country, the Kenyan police always pretended not to recognize it and therefore gave refugees a hard time.

As a consequence, during our journey to Nairobi, at every roadblock on the way, my group and I would be asked to get off the matatu (minibus) and would be taken to a room and thoroughly frisked. The search was not an exploration of weapons or other dangerous objects. It was for money. We were searched and sometimes almost stripped naked. While in these private rooms, I would negotiate with the police because the people who were travelling with me did not speak English. I would talk the police into accepting small amounts of money and letting us go. Sometimes I would give them 200 Shillings or less, depending on how well I negotiated. At times I would be threatened with being arrested if I didn't give them enough. Other times they tried to frighten us into giving them more money by letting our matatu go and leaving us behind.

The officer at Wilson Airport that day wanted me to remain in their custody, so I could pay a large sum of bribery in hard currency. I was the kind of a person the Kenyan police would get a lot of money from. Being in the company of white people implied that I must have access to lots of money.

In Kenya, money talks; everything is money. The Kenyan police work through a system of bribes. Thus, Southern Sudanese and other refugees were an extra source of shillings to the Kenyan police. When refugees, mostly Somalis, Eritreans, Ethiopians, Southern Sudanese, and other nationalities within Africa travel in a matatu in Kenya, they are consistently harassed by the Kenyan police and immigration officials until they arrive at their destinations.

Every so often, the police officers would plant contraband or bullets on refugees and accuse them of bringing drugs or weapons to Kenya. Those who were unfortunate to have this happen to them would be detained and required to pay a certain amount of money before being released.

Hope and Resurrection Secondary School

After this visit, the team returned to the United States to work hard on building a high-quality secondary school in the Rumbek region. We originally planned on raising $120,000 to build the school. However, we soon discovered that the real price tag would be closer to $300,000. We set out to raise the awesome sum of money, not completely convinced that we could even get close to our goal.

As it turned out, the fact that we had included a journalist on our trip to Rumbek made getting publicity for our cause relatively easy. A week after we got back from Sudan, in the Flair section, the *Richmond Times-Dispatch* ran Alberta Linsey's article in two parts: The first part was about life in Rumbek and the effect of the 21-year civil war, and the second part covered my family reunion in the villages of Titagok and Adol. The article came out in a Sunday paper, the most popular edition of the newspaper. To our surprise, many people started sending donations. Some sent personal letters telling me that they were touched by the story of my reunion in southern Sudan after years of separation.

It was about this time that Jennifer got a letter from an anonymous donor who asked many questions concerning our vision for the school and who, after honest answers to her inquiries, said she would match $25,000 if the organization would raise the same amount within three months of the agreement. The organization did, and she kept her promise. This was the largest single donation we ever received, and it brought our fund up to $90,000. Eventually, the same anonymous donor sent another letter offering another matching grant if we would raise another $25,000. We did, and she sent another check for $25,000.

After receiving these large donations, we were ready to find a good contractor to build the school. After searching for a few weeks, Jennifer got a phone call from Robert Claytor, the president of a South Carolina-based non-profit organization called Carpenters for Christ.

He broke the news that his organization was ready to take on the construction of the school. He added that an anonymous donor had donated $30,000 for the foreman's transport to southern Sudan, salaries and accommodations. I became very excited about the news because the dream of building a school in my village was coming true. Carpenters for Christ had just finished the construction of a clinic in Akot, just a few miles from Atiaba.

After years of anguish, I had brought something important to my people. It made me think of a common saying in Dinka that a "man goes to an unknown path but comes home on a known road." That was true in this case: I left home in a time of crisis to an unknown location but came home with something the community would treasure for generations. This saying in Dinka inspires the title of this book, Coming Home On A Known Road.

Within two months of the launch of the construction, the team from Christ Church and the board members of Hope for Humanity, Inc., including me, took a trip to southern Sudan and participated in the construction efforts. This was my second trip home. We could not believe how many people were waiting to welcome us at the airport.

I had also become a kind of hero among my Dinka people. It is believed there that young people easily forget about their families and places of birth when they find comfortable lives in different parts of the world. The Dinka people, as a pastoral community, also believe that when a child is kept in a cattle camp and goes through all the hardships of cattle camp life, that child will become strong and will never forget or abandon his people. They thought that during my early years in the cattle camp as a cattle herder, I was prepared to learn the love for my community, and that is why I did not forget about them.

Being from a prominent family, I was expected to work for the common good of the community. Bringing the school home to my people meant that I was fulfilling the community's expectations of me as well as my own dreaMs I was encouraged to keep doing good things for people across southern Sudan.

My Dream of Higher Education Comes True

Arriving in the U.S. without a secondary school certificate, the road to my college degree proved longer than I had imagined. I couldn't enrol in high school in the United States because of my age or be allowed to enrol in college without a secondary school certificate. So, my only option was to attain my General Education Equivalency or GED before a college would accept me. To get my GED, however, I had to study hard before I could take the test.

In early 2001, I started taking free English classes at the Second Baptist Church in Richmond, Virginia, and subsequently at Academy at Virginia Randolph. I also attended Refugee and Immigration-sponsored English and math classes at St. Mary's Catholic Church and the Jewish Community Center, but all were teaching below my level. I was required to be in these kinds of classes before I would be allowed to take GED exams, even though I had already taken a practice test and passed it.

I spent the whole of 2001 trying to figure out what to do to get into school. I felt like I was wasting valuable time. Some of my friends had already opted to go to Job Corps, where they hoped to obtain their high school diplomas, but I decided not to do that. It was a frustrating time for my friends and me, who were anxious to go to school but weren't allowed to.

In early 2002, however, a co-worker from The Mill Specialist (TMS) told me about J. Sergeant Reynolds Community College (JSR). He told me that he was taking some English as Second Language (ESL) classes there and that the school would accept me without a high school diploma. I asked whether the English classes offered there were good, and he said yes. The following evening after work, I went with him to JSR and registered. My boss at TMS had promised that the company would help pay part of my tuition. He gave me a check for one class. St. Bartholomew's Episcopal Church paid for another class and books. Despite the constraint that I must take only ESL classes and without financial aid, I was on the road to achieving my dream.

I worked hard, and all my instructors liked me. I was making friends among the teachers and students as well. This was the time when numerous articles were being written about me by the Richmond Times-Dispatch and other news outlets, and I also appeared on local TV stations, which made me well-known on campus. My personal story touched many people's hearts, and as a result, they were sending me cards of sympathy. Some would include checks in their cards and tell me to use them toward the cost of my education. I was getting the support I needed for my education and therefore was aware that my dream was coming true.

I requested a part-time position from my workplace, and it was granted. I wanted to work part-time, so I could concentrate on my studies. It was also a suggestion from the school financial aid office that I switch from full-time to part-time work so that I would qualify for a tuition grant.

At around this same time, an Indian couple, Sari and George Eapen, both medical doctors, who saw in the news that a local dentist had helped my roommate Peter with false teeth, called St. Bartholomew's Episcopal Church and asked to meet with the new refugees. Jennifer arranged for the meeting, and the Eapens came to our apartment the following evening. We shared a lot about our experience as refugees, and they told us about themselves and their experiences when they first arrived in America in the early 1970s. They asked how they could help and were told that education was our main goal. By that time, I was the only one of us going to school, and they promised to help me with my education. They continued their support until I graduated from Virginia Commonwealth University in 2007.

In May 2005, Patricia G. Satterfield (RIP) read an article about me and wrote me a very nice note saying that she was touched by the story. She included in her note a check for $1,000 for my education project in southern Sudan. She also came to support my education by paying for my books every semester until I graduated. Both the Eapen family and Ms Satterfield became like my family, and they would send me gifts during Christmas and invite me over to their homes for dinner. Both families continued to help my younger brother, who was going to law school in Kenya, with his education, after my graduation in 2007.

Once I completed the ESL classes, I enrolled in regular classes geared toward my ambitious plan for an Associate of Social Sciences degree. I had to take a wide range of classes which included math, science, history, political science, English, and a foreign language. I was required to complete more than 60 credit hours after prerequisite subjects before being awarded my Associate of Science in Social Sciences.

Though I was good in liberal arts subjects, math and science weren't my favourites. I had difficulty with math in particular and didn't like it at all. I took pre-calculus twice and dropped it twice because I couldn't understand it. I had been good at math in primary school but lost interest in it in the first year of secondary school. The third time I enrolled in pre-calculus, Jennifer Ernst hired a tutor to help me. In the end, however, I still got a C, but at least it allowed me to fulfil my requirement for graduation. I ended up having two C's in the two math classes required for my degree.

I was accepted into Virginia Commonwealth University in the fall of 2006. My first semester at VCU was difficult, in part because I was also finishing up two classes at JSR for my Associate Degree. I was taking seven classes, 19 credits in total, from two schools at three different campuses. Twice a week, I would come to VCU in the morning and then wait after my classes from noon to 7 p.m., then go to the JSR downtown campus for my biology class. Two other days of the week, I would go to the JSR Parham Road campus in the morning for my statistics class. It was a lot of driving, but I was excited. This has been my dream since childhood.

My first day at VCU was chaotic, to say the least. I came in the morning on a rainy day, and because I had failed to show up the week before for the tour of the campus and the orientation, I was in real trouble. First, I didn't know the location of my parking deck. It was 8:40 in the morning and my first class, Intergovernmental Relations, taught by Dr Nelson Wikstrom, was to begin at 9:00 a.m. at a location I didn't know.

For a while, I drove around, circling the campus, but finally decided to park my car in the Main Street deck when I couldn't find my designated location. I stepped out of the car and rushed to the street without an umbrella, and the rain was pouring on me. I tried to ask students on the street on the way to my class, but everybody was either running or walking in a rush to escape the rain. I went straight to the Student Commons, located in the centre of the campus next to the library, and I saw a sign that said, "Information Desk." I went straight there, pulled out my class schedule in a rush and handed it to someone. I showed her the class I wanted to go to, and she gave me a map of the campus, which wasn't helpful to me. She seemed to be new to the campus herself and didn't know much. Now, I was worried that I would miss my first class.

For the two years that I had been going to school in the U.S., I had never missed any of my classes, and I didn't want it to happen that morning. I was asking everybody I came across for help. Luckily, I eventually met a girl who was also taking that same class, and we arrived in the class 15 minutes late. I was soaking wet, but it was the least of my concerns.

As it turned out, the first day of the class was just an introduction and explanation of the policies that would govern the class. Nothing much! The professor introduced himself, and every student in the class did the same. The class was dismissed 15 minutes early, and I rushed out anxiously to find out the location of my next class. It was International Relations taught by Chris Saladino, a charismatic instructor whose class generated much interest in me and other students as well.

Fortunately, finding this class wasn't a problem because earlier, when I was looking for my assigned parking deck, I had driven down Main Street several times and seen the VCU Engineering Building where it was being held. I went straight to the building, and right next to the entrance was the class. I went in and sat in the second row. This was a lecture class; it had more than 100 students. The professor and his assistant were the only people to introduce themselves.

After leaving this class, I went straight to search for my economics class, which I found in the building next to the Student Commons. This turned out to be my least favourite class because it involved a lot of mathematical calculations, which I didn't like. After economics class, I would go back to the library until 6:30 p.m., when I would rush to JSR downtown campus for my biology class. I would be there in the class from 7:00 to 9:00 p.m. and then go home. The next day, I would be in school for the other classes in both schools.

Throughout the semester, I acquainted myself with the campus, making as many friends as I could. There were some other Sudanese students here, too; nine of them were Lost Boys. As time went by, I came to be involved with many presentations on Sudan and its worsening political and humanitarian situation in the region of Darfur. I was also involved with a documentary made by CBS in Richmond that was intended to encourage local lawmakers to push for a law prohibiting companies in Virginia from dealing with companies that had links with businesses in Sudan. I was also a member of the African Students Union (ASU). There were numerous articles written about me in *The Commonwealth Times*, the VCU newspaper.

I had a great interest in my Intergovernmental Relations class and was doing well in it. My professor, Dr Wikstrom, became my close friend and helped shape my political thinking. We talked about Sudanese and American politics and about the world at large. He would invite me for lunch, and we would spend most of our time talking about politics. He reenergized my decision to pursue my degree in politics, and all I thought about now was politics.

I kept myself busy at VCU, spending most of my time in the library, sometimes leaving at 2:00 in the morning. I studied hard and attended VCU basketball games. I graduated within a year and a half with a Bachelor of Arts in political science and a minor in criminal justice.

The School Dedication

In late March of 2008, our dreams of building a new secondary school finally took shape, and I returned with Jennifer, representatives from Hope for Humanity and church leaders to participate in the dedication on April 1st. It was an afternoon of scorching heat under clear skies. A crowd of people gathered under the shade of a gigantic tree in the middle of the school campus to celebrate the dedication of the brand-new secondary school built in the village of Atiaba in Sudan. Among this crowd were the community leaders, government officials, church leaders and representatives from Hope for Humanity, Inc. There were ululations amongst women in the crowd and singing as the two leaders, Mr Gordon Maker Abol, Lakes State Minister for Education, Science and Technology, and the Episcopal Bishop of the Diocese of Virginia, Rt. Rev. Peter Lee cut the ribbon to inaugurate the two modern building facilities for education in the village of Atiaba.

This ten-classroom school, Hope and Resurrection Secondary School (HRSS), would be the second secondary school in Rumbek, the fourth in the Lakes States and the twenty-second in the whole of southern Sudan. A crowd of people from church, community and government officials had travelled from far villages and towns such as Paloc and Rumbek to attend the official school opening ceremony. It was the day my community, Hope for Humanity, Inc. board members, the members of Christ Church Episcopal, and the Bishops from the Dioceses of Rumbek and of Virginia, whose relationship came through school construction, had all been eagerly awaiting.

The arrangements and preparations for the event were spectacular. There was great excitement amongst the community and organizations despite the temperatures of 40 degrees Celsius (104 degrees Fahrenheit) with high humidity. The first group of our team travelled to the school from Rumbek town on the evening of March 30 to prepare for the ceremony the next morning. That evening was also joyous as people from the churches and villages along the main road turned out in great numbers to welcome us. They lined the road, waiting for us hours before our arrival. When they saw us approaching, they excitedly sang church songs, beating drums made of animal skins and wood. Some danced on the road. Accordingly, we stopped to pray with the people and thank them.

I felt honoured by this and appreciated the people who had shown their love and gratitude for what we were bringing to them – a secondary school in their village. Our second team, which included Bishop Lee, was received the same way the next day of their arrival.

As everybody descended on the school campus, we could hear drums and singing in the distance. People were so excited to witness the grand opening of a secondary school in Atiaba because it was the first time in the history of the village to have a modern building with a tin roof. Too many people in Atiaba, this school was a sign of hope and prosperity for the people of southern Sudan after the devastation of a civil war that lasted for 21 years and left more than two million people dead and more than five million displaced.

For that reason, all the speeches delivered that day had one common theme; *bring back the hope for the future generation of southern Sudan through education*. The messages also carried with them appreciation because so few such projects have ever come to pass here

That day, I was very thankful for my connections in America, a country where people always say, "go for it if you think it is something you want to do." It's where people get behind you and encourage your ideas. After that magnificent day, I was inspired to continue doing many good things to help my people and prayed that God would help me to do more for my community and South Sudan.

At the end of that historic day, Jim and Mary Higbee from California took over the administration of the school. They were missionaries who were educators by profession and had decided to volunteer their time in southern Sudan and ensure that the school had a good start. They brought with them a 33-year-old Ugandan teacher named Cleous Bwambale. Four other teachers also from Uganda would join Bwanbale in the following weeks as the school began its admission process. Anthony Mading Wal from southern Sudan was hired as the headmaster of the school and was joined by two other southern Sudanese as part-time teachers.

I was impressed years later when I went back to what became the newest country in Africa, South Sudan, and visited the school in session. The school had grown in population from 66 students in 2008 to more than 300 students, with 109 of these as female.

South Sudan has not traditionally supported a female's right to education. According to UNICEF, fewer girls are educated in South Sudan than in any other country in the world. Less than one per cent complete primary education, and only one school-aged child in four is female. For our school to have more than 30 per cent of females was trailblazing. The retention rate for our female students was also high compared to other schools in the area, even though some of them are married off early by their parents.

Since the opening of our school, only two female students who were forced to marry by their parents dropped out of school between 2010 and 2011. One was tragically beaten to death by her parents when she became pregnant out of wedlock. However, despite that tragic death and the continuation of forced marriages, we were making great progress in providing quality education to our students.

Working after College

After years of struggle and hardship, I graduated from Virginia Commonwealth University in 2007 with a Bachelor of Arts degree in political science and a minor in criminal justice, a year and a half after obtaining an Associate of Science in social sciences degree from J. Sargeant Reynolds Community College. I had also accumulated more than $35,000 in student loan debt. My reason for burying myself in such astonishing debt was that my $700 monthly income from my part-time job at Walmart wasn't enough to cover all of my needs and expenses and also support my family back in Africa.

Most of my friends dropped out of school because of the family's endless demands back home. Culturally, it was always expected of any member of the family to cater to other family members if he or she was able to. For this reason, they would vow semester after semester to resume their studies after fulfilling their family's obligations, but they never did because more demands kept coming up, and they wanted to solve all of them.

For this reason, I decided to do it differently. I accepted the student loan given to me, so I was able to meet my family's demands from home and continue my studies without interruption. I also had credit cards which I used when I did not have money and paid off when I got paid from my part-time job.

Despite huge debts after graduation, I never regretted my decision because I believe that I achieved two targets at the same time: I relieved my family from their severe poverty and obtained my college degree. I hoped that with my education, clearing debts accumulated while in school wouldn't be a problem.

During my final year in college, my expectations were high. I hoped that soon after my graduation, there would be a job waiting for me out there where I could make good money and clear my debts within a few months. I had planned to work for one or two years and pay off my debts before I proceeded to law school, but the dream never materialized. My calculations were wrong because I could not find such a job anywhere in Virginia. It took me three painful years to finally find a job that I loved.

Throughout these three difficult years, I would apply for more than 50 jobs a week on the internet or on job sites but would hardly ever hear back. Only a few would respond to my applications through letters, usually telling me that they regret to inform me of their decision not to hire me for lack of qualifications. I would often ask myself why companies would expect a fresh college graduate to have the job experience they want.

Despite working full-time at Walmart after graduation, I was not happy with my job because it wasn't using the skills I attained in college, and I wasn't gaining any useful experience. I was doing the same manual job as those who never went to college. I would be sent out to collect shopping carts in the parking lot in all kinds of weather, wondering why I had worked so hard to obtain a college education.

I used the internet, newspapers and friends to search for job openings. One afternoon as I was sitting in the Walmart break room, I saw a *Richmond Times-Dispatch* newspaper on the table. I picked it up and quickly went through it, from the news to the advertisements. There, I came upon a notice of a job opening. It said the Obama campaign headquarters in Richmond wanted people to join the team. If interested, please call this number for an immediate interview and job placement. The compensation would be $10-13 an hour. As someone who had a degree in political science, I thought it was a great opportunity for me to join the campaign team and put my knowledge into practice. I took out my cell phone from my pocket and dialled the number immediately.

Someone answered and said, "This is Robert from the Obama campaign headquarters in Richmond. How can I help you?"

I explained, "My name is Maker Marial, and I am calling about the job advertised today in the *Richmond Times-Dispatch* newspaper."

"Please tell me about yourself," he said.

I responded, "I graduated in December 2007 from Virginia Commonwealth University with a Bachelor of Arts in political science and a minor in criminal justice after obtaining an Associate of Science degree in social science."

Before I could finish, he interrupted and said, "You don't speak good English, sir," and then hung up. I called back to ask why he said that, but someone else picked up the phone and told me he had just stepped out.

I was sad to know that I was being denied a job because of my accent. It was a sad moment not because I didn't get the job but because it was my accent that prevented me from getting a job, although I was more than qualified. The advertisement said they just needed college students for the job while I already had my degree. It was a story many of my friends and coworkers couldn't believe when I recounted it to them time and time again. Many of my friends and coworkers encouraged me to call again and explain the problem to someone higher up in the organization, but I said no. I didn't want to call and complain about being discriminated against. I believed there were other places where I could find a job.

One evening, after two years of unsuccessful job search, my friend Lilly Andrews invited me over for dinner with her family. She had been one of my closest friends since I got to America. I had travelled with her husband, Ron Andrews, to southern Sudan in 2007 for a mission trip to participate in a construction of a secondary school in my village of Atiaba. We had been good friends and members of the same church, Christ Church Episcopal, in Glen Allen, Virginia. As we were sitting at the dinner table, Lilly suggested that I should see whether there was any internship position available in the office of the Virginia Attorney General, Bob McDonnell. Lilly herself worked there as an assistant to the Attorney General. I had worked briefly in 2007 as an intern for the Richmond Commonwealth's Attorney's office headed by Mark Herring. Working under the supervision of Alex Taylor, the prosecutor for the Commonwealth's Attorney's office, I had gained some experience that Lilly believed would be valuable at the Attorney General's office.

The following morning, Lilly asked someone in the human resource department about any job openings or internship positions. She was told that there weren't any but that I should write a letter directly to Attorney General Bob McDonnell and express my desire to work in his office as an intern. I was very sceptical because I thought it wouldn't be wise to write to someone in the higher authority and ask him for a job that was not available. It seemed strange, but she was very persuasive and said that I should send her the letter first for review before sending it to the Attorney General.

I drafted the letter and sent it to Lilly. She made a few changes and sent it back. Now, the letter was ready to be posted. I later decided against sending the letter. I felt that it was presumptuous of me to write to someone as important as the Attorney General asking for a job when I had been told that there was no open position.

At this time, I wondered if my education would be better put to use in my homeland or in a country overseas. Working in southern Sudan would allow me to help my people who had been adversely affected by two decades of conflict in the country. I could also be a valuable asset to an organization there because I could speak some of the local languages, Dinka and simple Arabic (Juba Arabic) in particular. I searched on the internet and applied for several positions with USAID, Samaritan's Purse and other well-funded organizations doing humanitarian work in southern Sudan. The only organization that I heard back from was Samaritan's Purse, which sent me a nice note telling me that I didn't qualify for the position. The response was encouraging though I didn't get the job. It motivated me to continue applying for jobs.

My Way to the Senate of Virginia

As my job hunt had turned out to be unsuccessful, I gave up and concentrated on my job at Walmart. It was an unpleasant job, but by now, I was making $11.10 an hour and was able to pay my bills. I was working hard to protect my position. Additionally, I applied for other positions within Walmart, including supervisory and management positions in different departments and in other stores, but I wasn't successful. I continued to work in customer service, dealing with all kinds of customers. It was stressful and hard to handle, but it was the only thing I had at the moment.

Working in customer service, I would do a lot of different things, including MoneyGram money transfers. My former political science professor, Dr Nelson Wikstrom from Virginia Commonwealth University, would come in with his wife Anita to send money to the Philippines. Anita was from the Philippines and still had relatives back home. Apart from being my professor, Dr Wikstrom also became my close friend and would invite me for lunch occasionally when I was still at VCU. We would talk about U.S. and Sudanese politics, and it was a cordial friendship. Every time he came to the store, Dr Wikstrom would ask me whether my job search was coming along well, and I would say there is no progress. He would leave in disbelief.

One afternoon as I was still working my shift at Walmart, Dr Wikstrom again invited me to lunch. Dr Wikstrom told me that he would love for me to find something with the General Assembly of Virginia, where I would see what I had learned in the classroom being put into practice. "How can I find a job there, sir?" I asked. "I have a friend there named Jack Austin; you can call him and tell him that Dr Wikstrom gave you his telephone number. I know he will help you find something," Dr Wikstrom said. He then wrote down Jack's number on a piece of paper and gave it to me.

Two days passed while I was busy with work, but on the third day, I called, and Mr Austin answered. I told him my name, the reason for my call and how I had acquired his number. He was excited when he heard the name Dr Wikstrom. He later told me that Dr Wikstrom was his best friend. He said that he didn't know of any openings in his department but wanted my resume in case he heard of something in other departments. He gave me his email address, and I sent him my resume. He also told me that I should call the Clerk's Office and tell them that I want to find something like an internship position in their office.

On Friday, October 16, 2009, I called the Senate Clerk's office. Rose Ramsey, the secretary to the Clerk of the Senate, answered. She said she wasn't sure about any internship position available but suggested that I should write a letter to the Clerk of the Senate, Susan Clarke Schaar, and ask her for a job. After hanging up with Ms Ramsey, I realized that writing a letter to ask for a job must be something special in the American culture. I modified the letter I had drafted for the Attorney General and sent it to my friend Lilly Andrews for review. She sent it back to me that same day with a few recommendations. I mailed the letter the following day.

I had long since given up on a job in state government when, on Dec 18, 2009, I heard my phone bleep. I looked down and saw a message regarding an interview at the Virginia State Capitol. John Garrett, the Chief Deputy Clerk of the Senate, had asked me to check my email and call him back as soon as possible to schedule an interview.

As soon as my shift ended, I clocked out and headed home, eager to read Mr Garrett's email. According to his email, I was being considered for a temporary position during the 2010 Senate session, which was from January 11 through March 13. Despite it being a temporary position, I was willing to risk my full-time position at Walmart. I wanted a job where I could gain some experience, as many jobs I had applied for cited lack of experience as the major reason for not hiring me. Additionally, I believed that it would be an opportunity for me to interact with others who might offer me a permanent job.

On Wednesday, December 30, at 9:45 a.m., dressed in a grey suit, blue shirt, red tie, and brown shoes, I arrived at Capitol Square. I drove straight to the Capitol police kiosk located at the base of the George Washington equestrian statue. As I pulled in closer to the kiosk, a kind gentleman who was stationed there asked me where I was heading. I said that I was going to the Capitol for an interview with John Garrett. He checked my driver's license. I asked him for a parking pass as instructed by Mr Garrett. He showed me how to get to the gravel lot to park my car. I called Mr Garrett, and he came out to get me.

Mr Garrett took me on a tour of the Capitol and showed me all of the historical sights, statues and different offices, including the Senate Clerk's Office and what used to be the Governor's office. He also showed me the portraits of Virginia's former governors, lieutenant governors and senators. Remarkably, one of the portraits was of Julian Sargeant Reynolds, Virginia's former Lieutenant Governor, who passed away before the end of his term. My former college, J. Sargeant Reynolds Community College, was named after him. I never imagined I would be seeking a job where he used to work.

As we continued with our tour, Mr Garrett explained the history behind each site, statue and portrait. The tour was eye-opening for me. It ended in the Senate chamber, where I was shown many more portraits and the seats for the President of the Senate, Lieutenant Governor William Bolling, the Majority and Minority Leaders of the Senate, the Clerk of the Senate, Deputy Clerks, Calendar Clerk, and Counsel/Assistant Journal Clerk, and, finally, what would be my seat if hired.

I followed Mr Garrett into a small room which he told me used to be the kitchen, but it had been remodelled into something like a dining room. It was small but beautifully furnished with stunning sofas and chairs. "This is where Senators eat their lunches and hold small meetings during a session," Mr Garrett told me. Here, my other interviewers introduced themselves to me. The welcome was especially warm and friendly, and as a result, I felt relaxed throughout the interview. Indeed, that same afternoon, Mr Garrett called to offer me the job. The opportunity that I had been looking forward to for many years had now come my way. I would start work the very next morning, January 11, at 8:30 a.m., the first day of the General Assembly's 2010 session.

The session began at 10:00am, and I was amazed to witness such a colourful opening as the Lieutenant Governor, William Bolling, called the session to order and presided over the business of the day while the Clerk of the Senate called the calendar. As is traditional, on the first day of the session, the Clerk of the Senate called the names of all Senate pages and messengers and the Senators they were assigned to while parents and citizens looked on from the gallery. Each page or messenger would rise from the benches behind the Senators to be seen by the members, and there would be applause. After that, the Clerk announced the business the next day, and the members voice-voted approval for the adjournment of the session until the next morning.

Meanwhile, Ginny Edwards, Counsel/Assistant Journal Clerk, was busy with her keyboard, trying to catch every word that was said on the floor. She was responsible for recording legislative actions, managing floor votes and vote statements, preparing paperwork relating to bills and resolutions, and compiling data for the Senate Journal, Senate Manual, Faces of the Senate, and other publications. I was assigned to help Ms Edwards with all of these duties. She became my mentor. She explained things in a way that made it a lot easier for me to understand what she was teaching me.

Nathan Hatfield, Legislative Information Officer/Calendar Clerk, carefully followed the Senate Clerk during each daily session as she went through the calendar. Mr Hatfield projected the information for display on the four screens in the Senate Chamber. I tried to take in all this information at once, but it was overwhelming.

The first week was the week of pre-filing bills, in other words, bill introduction. I was very much involved with this process: I had to check all the draft bills for required senators' signatures, number them, and place them in shucks. These bill books would then be placed on each member's desk, so he or she knew the bills being debated on that day. Each day, after the session adjourned, I helped Mr Garrett and Mr Hatfield prepare the next day's calendar.

Staff members taught me how to prepare the journal, the calendar, and many other things that I needed to learn in my new job. I was shown where and how to deliver communications between the House and the Senate chambers. I really enjoyed this task as I walked between the two chambers passing by all the senators and the members of the House of Delegates.

As the session continued, the Clerk of the Senate stood up and gave a brief and kind speech about me and the reason why she decided to hire me to work in the Senate. She briefly narrated my background and how I got to America. Her words were followed by rounds of applause from the Senate as well as from the spectators in the gallery. It was a great honour! A lot of people in the Senate, in the gallery and even the Lieutenant Governor himself, hadn't known anything about me.

Representatives from both the pages and messengers called me to join them on the floor. A few days before, I shared with them my personal experiences and the work I was doing to help the people of southern Sudan. It was eye-opening to them, and they couldn't believe how I survived all the challenges along the way as I fled my country during the war in the late 1980s. My presentation moved them a lot, particularly after they had seen the video and the pictures about my school in southern Sudan. After that, the pages and messengers were motivated to contribute to my school project in southern Sudan and pulled together $120. They had also designed a beautiful poster signed by all of them. They presented the money, and the poster as the senators and the public in the gallery witnessed it. I was also given a check for $500 by the Senate. The event was televised across Virginia. I couldn't believe the overwhelming honour.

As I prepared to leave for a visit to Africa later in March, there was another surprise. This time it was from the Senate employees. The Clerk of the Senate had invited Senate employees to make contributions to my school project in southern Sudan. It was done strictly in secret, and I didn't know anything about it until I received a phone call from the Clerk's Office that I should come down to the Senate chamber. After everyone had gathered in the Senate chamber, Ms Schaar called me to the front and told me that the reason she had assembled everybody there was for my farewell party. I was leaving the next day. Then she handed me the envelope with all the checks for donations. I was blown away by such generosity. The contributions came to more than $1,300. Though I was left nearly speechless, I tried my best to thank all the employees for their kindness and generous gifts. Jennifer Ernst, Hope for Humanity's president, could not believe it when I delivered the envelope with all the checks in it to her.

Working in the Senate was a lot of fun and educational. The debates over the legislation were usually intelligent, civil and not directed to individual members of the Senate. During the debate, a member would push a button for a chance to speak from his or her desk, and the Lieutenant Government would kindly grant the floor for speech. Although they disagreed sharply on some issues, members of Virginia's Senate worked together to achieve common things for the benefit of all the citizens in the Commonwealth of Virginia.

Although my time at the state capitol was short, it fulfilled a childhood ambition of mine to be a lawyer and help people reach a consensus on divisive issues. It brought back memories of sitting at the feet of my great-uncle, who was the village chief. His wise counsel helped resolve arguments in my childhood community.

Village Governance in South Sudan

As a boy growing up in the village of Karic, I always dreamed of becoming an attorney. This was inspired by my great-uncle, Makuac Ater Marial, and his son, Ater Makuac Ater, both of whom were chiefs of Dour-Mayar clan. Chiefs in Sudan are like judges. They listen to both sides in the case and then decide on who is right and who is wrong.

My great-uncle Makuac Ater was young when he took over his half-brother Benyok Ater's chieftaincy. He later married twelve wives with whom he produced a sizeable number of children. Likewise, his son Ater was also married to five wives and had quite a number of children. Each chief was democratically elected by their clan members who stood in line behind them after every four-year term. There was no limit to how many terms they could serve. They were re-elected each time they ran because they were doing well in the eyes of their community.

Makuac was blind and always needed somebody to lead him to court every time he went to try cases. When I was as young as 4 or 5, I would often be the one to take him to court. I would grab his cane and lead him to a huge mahogany tree in the middle of the village and show him his gigantic wooden and bamboo chair. I would then sit beside him and listen while he tried cases. He had about five other junior chiefs known as bany-koor, with whom he worked to deliver good judgments. His judgments were always fair and highly respected, and he believed in truths.

While my great-uncle held court, I would sit calmly and listen carefully to the cases. The cases were mostly civil and marriage-related settlements. Seated between the plaintiff and defendant was an agamlong, an interpreter who repeats every word said in court loudly so that everybody could hear it clearly. This was part of transparency and fairness in the court. All court cases were open to the public, and everybody has a right to come to court and listen. They also have the right to make comments on the court proceedings.

My great-uncle was a lovable man. He would tell jokes in court to motivate people to listen to his cases carefully without being bored. He was also a great philosopher who predicted people's futures. He foretold the Sudanese conflict, which claimed the lives of more than two million people.

My Dinka Marriage

On the occasion of my visit to Sudan to witness the school dedication, I made the unexpected acquaintance of the woman who would be my wife. The school I helped build was being inaugurated in the village of Atiaba. Three young girls who became the pioneer students at this new school had joined the jubilant crowds. I came to say hello to them after the celebrations.

Social events like this are ideal places in the Dinka culture where young people meet each other. This is where friendships begin and sometimes end up in long-term relationships. Parents with marriageable sons would often scan the crowds for beautiful girls. The hunt for brides begins at special events like this.

However, I didn't look at these girls as potential brides. They were just students. I saw two of them had watches on their wrists and one didn't. I had brought several watches with me from the U.S. as gifts for friends and family and offered to give her one. The following day, I gave the watch to my cousin to deliver to her.

I went back to the United States after two weeks in southern Sudan. A few months later, I received a beautiful thank you letter from the girl. She expressed how excited she was after I gave her a watch she had not even asked for. The Dinka people appreciate gifts, especially when they are unexpected.

After reading the letter from her, I was moved, mainly because it surprised me that she showed her appreciation for my gift by sending a note thousands of miles across the ocean. My heart was touched greatly. Angelina's positive reception of the watch led me to discover what kind of a person she was. I wanted to reply to her letter in a special kind of way. The following year, I sent her a digital camera as a way to tell her that I appreciated her thank you letter. She cherished the gift and sent back another beautiful letter which I equally treasured. At this point, we both became friends but living in two different worlds.

At home in Atiaba, my family and relatives were contemplating my marriage. They were looking at different girls in Atiaba and in surrounding villages for my bride. My marriage had been of great concern for my family. Marriage is an obligation in the Dinka culture. Every male is expected to have a family and can marry as many wives as possible. My parents were worried that I would never be wed because my two brothers and a sister who were younger than me were already married and had children.

The Dinka culture does not allow for sibling lineage to be broken by allowing brothers or sisters to bypass each other in the line of marriage. Although an exception in this strict culture exists for girls, who are married off at early age to bring wealth in bride price to the family so her brothers can get married, still it's not easily allowed.

My parents were not happy that I was bypassed in marriage by my younger brothers, and they wanted me to marry immediately. My mom would always break into tears when I told her that I wanted to finish school before getting married. For years I resisted their demand. In 2009, two years after I graduated from college, I told them that I was ready to get married, and they were free to help choose my bride.

Two of my childhood friends suggested a woman that I had never met. It is common in Dinka culture for friends to choose a bride for a friend. She was in school somewhere outside the country. She sounded like a good prospect since I knew her parents as influential people in the community.

My family invited relatives and friends to their house to help them make the right choice. One of the women they proposed was my Angelina. Because she was one of our students at Hope and Resurrection Secondary School, I had not thought of her as a marriage prospect.

In 2009, I went to Rumbek to meet with the women and determine whether we felt a mutual connection. The first woman was living outside the country but came to Rumbek for the holidays. I thought Rumbek would be an ideal place to meet. Seeing her for a few days in Rumbek led me to understand that she wasn't meant for me.

During that time, I also visited with Angelina, and she treated me very well and with enormous respect. However, the whole time I was there, I didn't tell her my intentions. I arrived at her parents' house, and she welcomed me warmly. I wasn't sure whether she was aware of my parents' proposal to marry her.

I realized after that trip that Angelina was the person I wanted to spend the rest of my life with. I returned to Sudan once more in April of 2010, and this time I planned to inform her of my desire to marry her. I spoke to my brothers and cousins about my final choice of Angelina, and they agreed. Two days after my arrival, we went to Angelina's parents' house and proposed marriage to her, and she willingly accepted. It was great news for me because knowing her for two years convinced me that she was the right person.

After a month in Rumbek, I returned to the United States and left my family to prepare for the marriage. This included a headcount of the number of cows the family had, inviting relatives and friends to the house to inform them of the engagement, and determining how many cows each relative would contribute to the marriage.

Cows are central in Dinka marriage. The number of cows the boy's family has is what qualifies him to marry the girl he loves. Relatives and friends who are potential contributors to his marriage first ask to know how many cows the boy and his parents have when they propose marriage. This is called, in Dinka, *Lhok yi yo* (clean your chest). This means that the relatives will only contribute their cows to the marriage when the boy and his parents have several cows in place when they propose marriage. The boy must pay dowries to the girl's parents to compensate them for losing their daughter to another family. The girl is an industrious member of the family who performs many duties such as pounding grains, cooking, fetching water and doing other chores for the family. Accordingly, when parents give their daughter away, they expect her to perform similar duties for her husband and his family, and therefore they would want to be compensated for losing their daughter to another family.

My family and I had been preparing for this. I had saved and sent money home for years to buy cows. My brother was also doing the same, using the little money he had been saving from his job to buy more cows. My family was now ready, and the bride's family was informed of my family's intention to present a marriage proposal to them. My family was welcomed to the bride's family house, where the marriage proposal was announced and graciously welcomed. This process is called *thuot* (engagement announcement).

After the engagement announcement, Angelina's family set the bide price at 100 cows (the equivalent of $50,000) for the marriage. The dowry differs from one Dinka section to the other. It ranges from some tens (Upper Nile) to a few hundred in Bahr El Ghazal. Angelina and I belong to the Bahr El Ghazal Dinka agar section.

For a Dinka man to think of marriage, he must be ready to give cows to prospective in-laws. The bride price is negotiated by both families. These negotiations are the most difficult and interesting part of the Dinka marriage process. These talks are normally prolonged discussions between the bride and the groom's relatives, which could go on for more than a year.

Sometimes competition takes place when two or more men want to marry the same girl. Each one of them may offer more cows to outbid others. The girl's family or relatives would go around seeing the cows of each potential groom to make an informed decision about which man and his cows they would accept in exchange for their daughter. Thankfully, I didn't have to face such fierce competition with my marriage!

My family and friends accepted the price of 100 cows and divided the bill amongst themselves. They worked hard over the next several months to raise nearly 100 cows from uncles, brothers and friends. I also worked hard in the United States to raise money for a number of cows. I was lucky to have gained enormous support from my American friends, particularly Jennifer and Darryl Ernst, who I called my American parents. They sent a letter to their families and friends asking for contributions toward cows for my marriage.

My boss, Ms Schaar, gave me money for one cow. Ms Schaar got the word about my fundraising for buying cows for the dowry from Ms Patricia Satterfield, a good friend of mine who has always been there for me in times of need. She also contributed a cow to my marriage. She was delivering a check to me when she met Ms Schaar and told her of an interesting story of my fundraising for dowries to pay for my bride at home in South Sudan.

Social factors in Dinka culture determine the number of cows to be paid. These include the social status of the families and the education of both the bride and groom. Angelina's father held a high position with the South Sudan Police Service (SSPS). He was also of a high-class family based on his family's social status. My family also comes from a high social class. My father was a successful businessman before the war, and he became a famous soldier during the war. My great-grandfather was the paramount chief of the area, and my uncle now serves as the executive chief of Atiaba Payam (Payam is an administrative division below county).

I graduated from college in the United States while Angelina was a senior at a local high school. According to Dinka culture, this drives the bride price up to several hundreds of cows. A chief's daughters bring in more cattle to the family in the same way a chief's son is expected to pay more cattle for his wife. The more educated either the bride or groom is, the more cows the groom's family pays in bride price.

After all dowry price was met, Angelina Lella Makur, whom I accidentally met at the dedication of the school in Atiaba on April 1st, 2008, became my lovely wife in February 2011.

133

Independence Day in Juba[1]

As the world's newest country, we became Africa's 54th nation. "'It's a shout of freedom,' said Alfred Tut, lifting his head back and screaming," remarks Peter Martell of the BBC News, reporting from Juba that day. Shouts and screams for happiness were the mood in Juba the night before and during Independence Day. I was one of the noisy and excited South Sudanese. It was sound pent up for generations as our long-awaited nation was being born in East Africa. Its birth seemed to mark the end of slavery, war, destruction, disease, starvation and oppression from the Arabs and Islamists in the north.

A gigantic digital clock erected in central Juba counted down the remaining hours, minutes, and seconds to the anxiously awaited day. Juba was where most celebrations would take place. Vehicles packed with people waving the multi-coloured and beautiful new nation flags toured the streets, honking horns in celebration. "Congratulations, free at last, South Sudan," the script on the digital countdown clock read.

South Sudan's independence concluded nearly 50 years of political struggle and social liberation against the marginalization and the forceful imposition of Islamic and Arabic ideologies on the black Africans in the south by the Arabs in the north. Defending their rights, southerners took up arms to defy several successive regimes in Khartoum from 1955 through 1972 and again from 1983 through early 2005. These civil wars were a result of Arabs' repeated deception, abuse, neglect and attempts to coerce black Africans to abandon their cultural beliefs and adopt those of Arabs. It was a genocide.

The first destructive civil war, which lasted for 17 years, started in 1955, one year before Sudan gained its independence from the British and ended with an agreement signed in Addis Ababa, Ethiopia, in 1972. The outbreak of this war was a result of southerners' reaction to

---

[1] The referenced article can be found at *https://www.bbc.com/news/world-africa-14091903*

the British's decision to grant independence to Sudan as a united country instead of granting the north and south their individual independence. Southerners believed then that the great inequalities between north and south, exacerbated by Britain's "Southern Policy or the Closed District Ordnance" for administering the south, were so wide that they preferred to be independent. Under the Closed District Ordnance, the south was closed to outsiders, northern Sudanese in particular, under the pretext that it was 'not ready for exposure to the modern world.' This resulted in the underdevelopment and backwardness of the south, and the southerners opted for integration into East Africa, when Sudan gained its independence as a consequence.

However, their choice was not honoured, and the result was war. This civil war continued for 17 years and ended with the Addis Ababa Peace Agreement in 1972. The Addis Ababa Peace Agreement did not last long, though. It was dishonoured when the regime in Khartoum declared Sudan an Islamic state. And what would become the most brutal and longest-running civil war in Africa broke out in May of 1983, after ten years of relative peace, and continued for 21 years. This most dreadful and painful war left approximately 1.5 million, mostly southerners, dead and more than 5 million displaced from their homes. This second civil war ended with the intervention from the international community, notably the United States, Norway and the UK, when the peace agreement, which paved the way for South Sudan's independence, was signed in the Kenyan capital, Nairobi, on January 9, 2005. This peace agreement gave the people of southern Sudan the right to vote in a referendum for secession. During six days of voting that ran from January 9-15, 2011, more than 98 per cent of Southern Sudanese overwhelmingly voted for secession. The 2% who voted no for the independence were those who were in Khartoum and did not want the country to break into two.

The Southern Sudanese came out in big numbers to celebrate the independence of their new nation in Juba, throughout the south and elsewhere around the world, where Southern Sudanese sought refuge during the war.

Two hours before midnight, cars loaded with mostly young people whizzed around Juba town, each blaring out a different tune. The independence of South Sudan means total freedom from the northerners' oppression.

"We have waited too long for this special day, so we cannot sit indoors," Atem Garang told Peter Martell of BBC News. "I have come out because I cannot believe we have arrived at this point of a new nation after such a long, hard road of fighting," he said.

Roundabouts throughout Juba became hyperactive dance venues when trucks mounted with giant speakers slowly passed by. "We are going, we are going to freedom," people sang in excitement. Women ululated while men chanted excitedly, "SPLA Oyee, SPLA Oyee," referring to the Sudan People's Liberation Army that had fought and won the right of Southern Sudanese to self-determination. Some triumphant Southern Sudanese were wearing the flag of their new nation draped around their shoulders while they chanted, "We are going to the promised land."

Cars of all sizes and kinds filled the streets of Juba. Those who could not fit inside the cars hung out the windows while others sat on the roofs. Many cars had stickers on them saying different things about independence. Some of them read, "Just divorced" and "bye, bye north." The atmosphere in Juba was wild. Church bells rang during the midnight hour but were quickly drowned out by the deafening sound of horns and other instruments coming out of other parts of the city. Groups of people were dancing to the drumbeats that sounded everywhere and running down the roads. Soldiers and police officers joined in. Many of them had fought with the Sudan People's Liberation Army (SPLA). "I fought with the SPLA, and now we have won," Gony Thon told BBC News.

Families and friends who did not want to go on the streets organized their own small parties at their homes and feasted on roasted goats they had prepared for the celebration. These kinds of celebratory parties went on throughout the night and into the next several days.

Apart from feasting on roasted goats for celebration, many lit candles in memory of family members killed and all those who lost their lives during the war. There had been an official announcement from the government that at midnight people would go to churches and light candles in memory of those who perished during the war, and many citizens answered the call. "I light candles in church when I say a prayer," said Alice Ajak, a mother who lost two children during the long years of war, speaking to BBC News. "My candle here, therefore, is my prayer that my new country is one of peace and where we can live without problems for now and in the future always to come," Alice further explained.

Juba International Airport was also busy. World leaders were arriving and being received by government officials. On the way to their accommodations, the visiting world leaders were greeted by groups of joyous Southern Sudanese who wanted to show their appreciation for the support they rendered during the war.

The official ceremony finally took place at noon. World leaders delivered speeches. The United Nations, African Union, European Union, Arab League and many countries worldwide were represented. Former Secretary of State Collin Powel represented the United States. Sudan was also represented by its leader Omer Hassan Al-Bashir who delivered a very important message in recognition of the break-away part of his country. Hundreds of media outlets worldwide covered the ceremony. After the speeches, military, police, prison, fire brigades, wildlife wardens' brass bands and wounded heroes formed a colourful parade at John Garang Mausoleum, the venue of the celebration.

Behind the crowds of thousands of people listening to the speeches were the traditional dancers who came to Juba from all over the country to celebrate the independence of their country. They danced to showcase the richness of Southern Sudanese culture. Everybody was in a celebratory mood except for the soldiers, who didn't sleep for three days as Juba geared up for the celebration. Soldiers were deployed to guard against those who would sabotage the celebration and put the lives of the citizens and invited guests at risk. They seemed tired and hungry but were always alert, and the celebration ended without a single incident.

I was there to celebrate the birth of a new country. I had wanted to be in the capital city for the celebration and was excited and thankful that I was able to be there for the historic independence of my country. I never thought it would happen in my lifetime. I grew up during the war and experienced all the ghastly things the war could bring to people.

Throughout wartime, hopes for peace were always eroding as peace talks took place and then broke down. Compromise seemed impossible. As a result, many people in southern Sudan came to believe that there would never be a peaceful settlement between Khartoum and the southern rebels. Hence, the signing of a peace agreement in 2005 was a big surprise.

Because people in southern Sudan did not have access to the internet or television, news of peace talks spread only by word of mouth through the villages. They were eager to see the end. Most people didn't even understand the reasons for the outbreak of the war. They were born into a culture of war and never knew anything different.

My grandmother, Achol Mayol Angaknhom, did not live long enough to see the end of the war. She was a big fan of peace talks news. Although she was illiterate and could not speak any other language except her native, the Dinka, she always tried to gather information about the peace talks taking place in foreign countries. She would then inform her neighbours about these developments.

Everyone in southern Sudan would be alarmed when they heard Garang's popular phrase "howon misimir", meaning bombs continuous, over the SPLA's radio. This is because when Dr John Garang, as he used to be called, released this phrase, he meant that the peace talks had broken down and that the war must continue. Garang was the rebel leader in southern Sudan who was fighting against the Arabs and Islamists regime in Khartoum.

As a consequence, the war would intensify in the days and months after the breakdown of the peace talks. I still do not know the reason why war always intensified when both sides disagreed and couldn't continue with the peace talks. Civilians were always the targeted victiMs

Witnessing the independence celebrations and the happiness among the Southern Sudanese in Juba made me proud of my father, Mabor Marial Benyok, that day. He had sacrificed everything important to him, including his family, to fight with the rebel movement in the early 1980s. He recruited many troops and captured and protected many Southerners who were caught fighting alongside the enemy. He fought in many battles throughout southern Sudan, including the failed attempt in 1992 to capture Juba, now the capital of South Sudan. He survived it all to witness the independence of southern Sudan. He was the first to lead his family to vote for separation in his home village of Atiaba on January 9, 2011. He also led his fellow wounded heroes in a military parade in Rumbek East County Headquarters, Aduel, on July 9, 2011, to mark South Sudan's independence. This parade was for them.

I was also proud of myself for registering and voting in the referendum that had led to the secession of southern Sudan from the north. I drove for two hours to Alexandria, Virginia, on January 9, 2011, and stood in a line in the freezing cold for about two hours before I finally cast my vote.

I was proud of being one of the Southern Sudanese who actively raised awareness about Sudan in the U.S. Before the Lost Boys and Girls came to the U.S., many Americans didn't know anything about our conflict in Sudan and, therefore, couldn't do anything to urge the U.S. government to bring an end to the war. The Lost Boys and Girls shared their personal stories in newspapers, TV interviews, documentaries, civic engagements, and books. Many Americans were inspired and pressured the U.S. government to intervene and bring the conflict to an end. Standing in line to vote that day was branded as "The Final Walk to Freedom." South Sudan's independence had been anticipated for decades. It was now a dream come true.

December 2013 Graduation from Virginia Commonwealth University (VCU)

On Saturday, December 14, 2013, I graduated from Virginia Commonwealth University (VCU) with a Master of Public Administration (MPA) from the L. Wilder School of Government and Public Affairs. This was my second graduation ceremony at VCU since I graduated in 2007 with a Bachelor of Arts in Political Science and Criminal Justice. However, this December 2013 commencement was special because I was one of the two students whose stories were shared by Michael Roa, VCU's president, with 2,800 students who were receiving their degrees that day and thousands of parents and friends who attended the graduation ceremony.

The first story was entitled, 'using knowledge as your greatest weapon in any struggle,' a story of Jason Newton, a staff sergeant in the U.S. Army Reserves. He was receiving his PhD in biochemistry from VCU's School of Medicine. He joined the Army after the Sept. 11, 2001, terror attack and was quickly deployed to Fallujah and Al Asad in Iraq, where he spent more than a year. After his deployment and return home, he joined a team from VCU that was dedicated to helping treat victims of traumatic injuries. This was inspired by his personal experiences in Iraq when he saw medical helicopters evacuating wounded soldiers for treatment and joined in to help. For this reason, Jason and his faculty mentors were inventing ways to make blood clot faster so death related to blood loss would be reduced. Jason's story was inspiring, and he received cheers from students as well as the graduation attendees.

The second story was mine. It was entitled, 'finding your way, even when all seems lost.' The college president's speech chronicled my earlier life in a village in Sudan amidst the brutal civil war and my struggle to get an education in a country where only 25% of children could enrol in school. He recounted the attack on my village and my journey to the refugee camps in Ethiopia and Kenya. He spoke of my struggles in the United States to complete my education. He concluded his speech by telling the audience about the school I helped build in South Sudan. The narration of this story was beautiful, and there were cheers from my colleagues, parents, and friends. I felt so honoured when many people later came to congratulate me after the ceremony.

I was supported by friends and family that day, and we had lunch together after the ceremony. My friend Lisa Thompson and her husband Bill took us out for lunch to celebrate this remarkable life achievement.

Since childhood, my dream was to go to law school and become an attorney. I even sat for an LSAT and got scores that could get me into some law schools; however, in 2010, I put off that plan and used my LSAT scores for admission to VCU instead. I was preparing to get married and had to work to save for the dowry. My hope was that I would still go to law school after having a family.

Unplanned Stay in Africa

In March 2014, I returned to Africa for two reasons: first, to meet my 13-month-old son for the first time since he was born and second, to finalize the process of bringing my family with me to the United States. I had filed an I-130, a family reunion immigration form, for my wife in 2012, and the process had been lengthy with a lot of paperwork. However, just after the immigration process was about to be completed, I received discouraging news from the Commonwealth of Virginia Senate Clerk's Office that my job would not be there after the new budget. The news upended my plans, and I had to think of how I would support my family. By that time, the U.S. Embassy in Nairobi, Kenya, was waiting for my family's passports to be mailed to them so a visa could be issued for my wife. My son already had his U.S. passport and did not need a visa.

After receiving the news that I would not have a job when I returned to the U.S., I worried that I might not be able to provide for my family back in the U.S.

I shared my job frustrations with my family, and they advised me to proceed to South Sudan, where I would most certainly find work. Although there were still pockets of ethnic fighting in the country, the economy had greatly improved. They felt that getting a job would not be a problem since I was a strong supporter of the government and someone with a great education from the first world. I took the advice seriously and contacted a friend of mine in Juba about my plan to visit the country. He offered to buy me an air ticket, and I flew to Juba.

Arriving in Juba in late May, I was received by brothers, relatives, and friends. They were all working for the government. They accommodated me and supported my family financially in Kenya while I looked for a job. My search for a job in Juba wouldn't be as easy as I had thought. It became difficult, and I was struggling. I soon realized that getting a job in South Sudan would require someone to have money to bribe people and relatives in the most powerful positions in the country. My brothers, relatives and friends were all working as junior civil servants since they were just fresh from college. They were not in high enough positions or had money to assist me. Meanwhile, NGO jobs were also not easy to get. They were politicized. Those in power felt the Dinka people were corrupt, violent and lazy. My name would easily identify me as Dinka, and my application would be discarded. I also had a problem with inexperience because I never had never worked for an NGO before. Added to that, I was viewed as an outsider and someone who did not know the country's context since I had been away for decades. It proved to be more of a challenge than I expected.

Meanwhile, my friends who did not have a good education in the U.S. or work experience outside South Sudan were quickly employed and driving SUVs popularly known in the country as V6s or V8s if they had relatives in the top positions in the government. They also had fat bank accounts and mansions in the country and outside South Sudan.

One day as I was walking in the street, I ran into a good friend of mine who also came from the west. He was employed and working for the ministry of water resource and irrigation. We quickly chatted, and he advised me to contact an uncle of his that had helped him find his job. He gave me his uncle's telephone number; however, the big man was not happy with my phone call. His first reaction was to question how I got his number in a deep, angry voice, and I told him. He then cooled down, and we talked and finally scheduled a place and time to meet and talk about my needs. However, when the time came, he did not show up at the venue and subsequently did not pick up my phone calls. I found out later from my friend that he had called soon after we hung up, and was very upset with him. He scolded him for giving me his telephone number as I was not a family member.

With that chapter closed, I contacted another friend of mine who worked in the office of the president and asked him to help me find a job. His response was that he would talk to one of the generals in

Bilpam, the Sudan People's Liberation Army (SPLA) headquarters, and see if he wanted someone with skills like mine to work for him. During that time, South Sudan's army had good-paying jobs since they were receiving more than 60% of the national budget. I gave him the go-ahead to do that, and he contacted one of the generals. Two days later, I received a phone call from him that I should prepare to go to a military intelligence training centre outside Juba for training before I could start work. He said I would graduate with the rank of captain and then be sent to a foreign country for further training before starting work. I was excited and prepared for it.

A week later, I received a phone call from the recruiter who told me the time and date for reporting. I reported on the date he had told me; however, I came late and missed the bus. I was very upset, but the recruiter advised me not to dwell on it. "Please go home, and I will call you when another opportunity comes up," he assured me. I thanked him and left, heading home. In my mind, that chapter had also closed, and I started contemplating my next attempt for a job in South Sudan.

By this time, things were getting difficult for me financially because I could not afford to pay for rent and food for the family in Nairobi. Since my brothers and friends were having their own financial challenges and could not continue to support my family. I moved my family to Juba to be with me as I looked for a job.

As I sat on the bus headed toward Juba, I received an unexpected phone call from Viable Support to Transition and Stability (VISTAS), a project funded by USAID. I had an interview with them a few months before for the position of program specialist, but it was given to another qualified candidate, and I was promised a position at the headquarters if there was an opportunity. Another opportunity for a position of grant specialist had come up in Lakes State. I was asked if I would be interested in the position, and I graciously said yes, though it was below my qualifications. I did the interview, but I was still doubting whether it would be given to me due to my lack of experience. The phone call I received was a job offer from this organization. I was excited and went straight to the office to sign the contract. I started a one-week orientation the following day and was dispatched to my field location – Rumbek - afterwards.

Arriving in Rumbek in January 2015, I found staff had confined themselves to the office because of the widespread insecurity caused by the intra/intercommunal violence and revenge attacks. There was only one project activity being implemented then, the Rup and Pakam Peace Dialogue. The two communities had been fighting a deadly conflict since 2012, and hundreds of people had lost their lives as a result. Almost all of the other communities in Lakes State were fighting each other either over control of land, access to water or mere misunderstanding among the communities. Lives were being lost as a result.

Consequently, insecurity was getting worse day by day, as many people were getting killed almost on a daily basis. This was worsened by the political and local leaders who were dividing people because of selfish interests. Road ambushes, cattle raiding, robbery, and revenge killings were rampant. Some policemen and army officers were also involved in these crimes. The government was failing miserably to control the situation, and there was a serious breakdown of law and order. Some NGOs, both international and local, including VISTAS and UN agencies, were trying their best to mitigate the conflicts, but it was not an easy task as people were being targeted for revenge attacks, and staff couldn't go out to interact with communities to help meet needs and heal the divisions.

Now being a new member of the team in the Rumbek VISTAS field office, I came with an American mentality and refused to be confined to the office. I was on the road almost every day, travelling in the most dangerous areas to meet with community leaders and discuss with them opportunities for peace and reconciliation in their communities. Most NGOs and commercial vehicles were getting shot at or robbed almost every single day, but I had the resolve to continue to move around despite this threat. I saw myself as neutral and somebody trying to reconcile the divided and warring communities and save lives. Consequently, I was getting known in the area, and nobody tried to stop my vehicle during those turbulent times.

As I settled in, most of our team members were going on leave. They had been in the field for a long time and wanted a break from all the daily bad news of Rumbek. Our program specialist Malok had written a proposal for bringing Rumbek's artists together for a peace messaging caravan which got funded. However, with the experienced staff on leave, I remained in charge of the office and the implementation of the peace messaging activity. I was nervous because I did not know how to begin. However, before Malok left, he showed me briefly what I should do, and I gained confidence.

A few days later, the artists started arriving in Rumbek, and I was picking them up from the airport and dropping them off at the hotels. I also started planning with them how the peace messaging should be implemented to achieve its intended goal. The aim of the peace messaging caravan was to restore hope after the widespread conflicts that had affected people badly, as many were forced to flee the town for safety reasons. The value of the grant was $40,000, and it was enough to fund all the activities in the project.

Two days before the peace messaging caravan, I hired four pickup trucks, mounted them with loudspeakers, and the artists went around town singing and playing music. They were also telling people about the upcoming peace concert at Freedom Square in Rumbek town. People could not believe what they were hearing because concerts or traditional dances were rare since the outbreak of intra/intercommunal violence in Lakes State.

On the day of the concert, hundreds of youths turned up, and the concert continued until it was 9:00pm without violence or anybody threatening peace. This was against the usual self-imposed curfew as people were always in fear of attack as revenge attacks were rampant.

The peace concert turned out well. I took beautiful pictures and wrote a nice article about the peace messaging caravan and sent it to my supervisor, our Regional Program Manager or RPM, Richard. He was impressed with it and immediately shared the report with our headquarters in Juba. It was the talk of the day as the report was also shared with USAID, which gave positive feedback. I wasn't aware until Richard called and told me about the positive reaction he was getting from our head office in Juba and the USAID to my report. I was motivated and encouraged by this and planned to create more peace projects and implement them.

I mapped out all the warring communities and studied the genesis of their conflicts and the impacts each conflict had on the communities. I wrote a report on the origin of all the conflicts I identified and shared them with my boss, who was impressed with how I explained each conflict with facts and statistical evidence. Proposals were developed and funded.

It was now February, and we were readying ourselves for the rollout of the project implementation. Our efforts coincided with the national agenda for peace in Lakes State. Intra/intercommunal violence in Lakes State had dominated the news for years, and both the national parliament and the government in Juba were getting tired of the sad daily news emanating from Lakes State. The presidency had funded the peace project, and the president himself came to launch it in Rumbek.

This was a perfect opportunity for us as a program. We invited the community's leaders to our office to sign MOUs for peace dialogues in their communities, and the peace delegates were soon brought to town to pave the way for community-level dialogues.

At first, we were nervous about putting all the participants together because of the animosity between the communities. However, I decided that they should be mixed and accommodated in the same hotel since they were brought to forge peace.

The next day, peace dialogues for greater Yek were initiated. Sons and daughters from the 4 communities who lived in Juba also attended. People talked from their hearts about how the conflicts had affected them and expressed willingness for forgiveness. I was happy to see how frank people were and could not wait for the outcome. When one chief said something that people regarded to be a hostile statement, he was criticized sharply by many, including his own people. This indicated that everybody was tired of the prolonged and deadly conflicts and wanted peace. The delegates returned home to sensitize the rest of their communities about peace while the peace committees were shuttling among the communities to ensure that people were following the resolutions from the launch.

We continued this process for other targeted communities, bringing them to town for the launch of their peace dialogues and returning them to their communities to continue with sensitization. Consequently, slowly a new calm was spreading throughout many areas.

There were some failures. The leaders of one group refused to support peace dialogues because they insisted that a man suspected of killing the chief be prosecuted and executed before the two conflicting parties could come together for peace dialogue. This fanned the flame of violence, and more lives were lost as a result.

We also organized an interborder peace conference in Aluakluak Payam in Yirol West County for the communities in Rumbek, Yirol West, and Yirol East Counties. This 5-day peace conference brought together youths, chiefs, community leaders, and government officials to discuss cross-border cattle raiding, road ambushes and retaliatory attacks. The meeting went well for the five days as participants expressed their willingness to forgive each other and live in peace. Resolutions from the peace conference were passed and signed by the community leaders and government officials. I was excited about this peace conference because my mom comes from Aluakluak while my dad comes from Rumbek East. I could not visit my maternal relatives because of the conflict the two communities had. For this reason, I was hoping for the Aluakluak Peace Conference to restore peace among the bordering communities so people like myself could move freely.

Unfortunately, though, some people with ill intentions were waiting on the outskirts of Aluakluak to strike after the conference ended because one of their relatives was killed by suspected youths from Aluakluak days before, and they wanted to avenge his death at that critical time.

After we concluded the talks, we put the participants in the vehicles and returned them to their various locations. I was returning to Rumbek with participants from Rumbek East County and staff while my colleagues were escorting the participants from Yirol East and Yirol West Counties to their locations. An hour after our departure, I received a terrible phone call that 2 participants, plus the boda-boda guy (motorcycle rider), had just been killed on their way home after the conference. One of them was my maternal cousin. I was very upset about the news. I also received the terrible news that youths from Aluakluak had ambushed our convoy on its way to Yirol town and Yirol East and wanted to kill our drivers to avenge those who had just been killed. It was a bad afternoon for me. They were only allowed to live when the Yirol West County Commissioner intervened and dispersed the youths from the road. It was a terrible experience. For a time, I regretted organizing the peace conference, which ended with the death of 3 people, including my relative. However, I convinced myself that for every failed attempt, we had set other communities on a path to peace. I continued with the peacebuilding activities.

It was now the end of June 2016, and I resigned from VISTAS and joined Catholic Relief Services (CRS) as its Project Manager in Rumbek. South Sudan Council of Churches had just been awarded $6.5 million for a 3-year peacebuilding project known as Reconciliation for Peace Project in South Sudan (R4P) by USAID through CRS. The project was to be implemented in Western Equatoria, Jonglei and Lakes States. I went to Juba for orientation with the hope of returning to my field location and starting my peacebuilding activities afterwards. Less than a week in Juba, however, war broke out between the current government and opposition forces.

When it appeared that South Sudan would descend into another civil war, all the International nongovernmental organizations (INGOs), including CRS, evacuated most of their international staff. The CRS Office in Juba was partially shut down. I stayed with my family in Juba for 3 months until the office reopened fully. However, after Riek's opposition forces left Juba and peace slowly returned to the city, I returned to Rumbek and started the implementation of the peace activities. I was organizing peace conferences for the warring communities to find peaceful means to address their issues. I was also supporting interfaith peace dialogues by bringing Muslims, Christians, and animists together to dialogue and agree to live in peace while practising their beliefs.

We implemented intertribal peace dialogues in Rumbek and Wau, Western Bahr El Ghazal State. In Lakes State, for example, we successfully encouraged Dinka Gok and Jur Beli to dialogue and reconcile their differences over a place called Ngap. The two tribes were contesting its ownership, and a deadly war broke out, which resulted in killings, destruction of properties and displacement of people. In Wau, we were supporting three tribes, Dinka, Fertit and Luo, to reconcile and live in peace. They were fighting over control of Wau town after the government's decision to relocate Wau County to a place called Bagari.

Our other peace activity was to support Rup and Pakam peace dialogue. The two groups had been fighting since 2012 when Pakam's ally, Kuei, had a deadly conflict with Rup after two members of the two communities had a disagreement over mosquito net stands that were borrowed and not returned. Fighting ensued between the two people, and it escalated to involve others, including youth from Pakam clan in support of Kuei. This conflict was deadly, as each encounter among the fighting groups usually left more than 100 people dead and hundreds of cows stolen. We tried to bring them together for dialogue when I was at VISTAS but failed.

However, with the new program, I strongly believed that we could have a breakthrough and save lives. Therefore, we brought together 40 youths comprised of youth leaders, chiefs, and politicians from the two communities in Rumbek town, so they could dialogue among themselves and find a solution to their problem. They agreed to reconcile and live in peace. They resolved to go back to their respective communities and sensitize people about what was agreed upon and the way forward to peaceful coexistence. We were excited and supported their roadmap for peace. We were going from cattle camp to cattle camp for consultations, and everything was going on smoothly. We were successful in making the two warring communities agree to settle their differences, return stolen cattle, and merge their cattle camps together. They also agreed to let go of those who were killed and live in peace without seeking revenge. Those who were displaced from their homes, mainly Rup, were to return home and live side by side with their former enemies. They did as agree, and months passed with tranquillity. No one had ever thought of making these warring communities agree to live in peace after years of deadly conflict.

However, our celebration was short-lived. With no warning, the worse violence erupted between the communities when the truce was violated by cattle theft. Over 120 people were killed that day, while many others were wounded. These included women, children, and the elderly. It was a sad day for us as a program because our greatest success had turned into an utter failure.

As a peacemaker in Rumbek, I became targeted by enemies. Other organizations that had the same peacebuilding projects as ours were not happy with the way we were implementing our project's activities.

We were giving our participants incentives whenever they participated in any of our project activities. We were reimbursing them for transport money and providing them with food and accommodation. Other organizations could not afford this, so people were not interested in participating in their activities. This became a conflict, and I was reported to the governor as someone working for the downfall of other NGOs in the state. Out of the blue, the governor ordered my arrest without giving me an opportunity to listen to my side of the story. In this culture, anybody with access to power has the ability to have someone arrested with or without cause. However, those he had ordered to execute his orders did not agree with him. They told him how I was changing their lives and the lives of their families through the incentives whenever they participated in any of our activities, which were frequent. It was difficult economically for the government's employees as states were divided, increased from 10 to 32, and the government's resources stretched to their limit. The local currency was also devalued, which also affected salaries. Consequently, the government's employees would go for months without being paid salaries. And if they were paid, the money would be valueless to buy anything from the market.

Our peacebuilding activities always involved government officials because they were the ones who helped coordinate our activities and worked with the communities to implement the resolutions. They relied on our funding to make it through these lean times. Failing to secure support for my arrest, he ordered I leave his state immediately. I informed CRS about the governor's decision, and I was flown to Juba, where I stayed for months while my project stalled. As time went by, some of his cabinet ministers fought for my return, and he agreed. I returned and resumed my work. The same people went to him again, and I was expelled for the second time. Although I was born and raised there, because I no longer had political influence, I could be thrown out of my own state.

While working for CRS, I was also supporting Hope and Resurrection Secondary School whenever there was a need for my support. There was a complaint that some people in the community were encroaching on the school's land. I went to local chiefs and community leaders and discussed the need for demarcation to curb the encroachment. It was agreed, and a team from the Department of Land, Survey, Housing & Public Utilities was dispatched to the school the next day to undertake the survey. However, when we arrived, the police would not allow the survey to be executed. They said that they were sent by the commissioner to stop the work because he wasn't informed about the survey and needed a letter from the office of Land and Survey before he could let the work continue. I returned to Rumbek with the team of surveyors and got the required letter from the director. We returned the next day and presented the letter to the executive director because the commissioner was not available. He gave us the green light to go ahead. However, as we were about to arrive at the school, I received a phone call that we were being followed by armed soldiers. The commissioner had sent them to arrest me after getting the letter from his executive director. He was very upset that we had returned. He was blocking this survey in response to my earlier refusal to support him during his campaign for commissionership. It was getting ugly quickly in Atiaba as soldiers arrived, and the local youths were getting their weapons and readying themselves to fight them. It was a chaotic scene as the local leaders, and we tried to control the situation before it became violent.

I returned to Rumbek with the team of surveyors and reported the matter to authorities, but they could not do anything to force the commissioner to allow the survey to resume. This commissioner enjoyed a close relationship with the governor and was very arrogant. He would not tolerate anyone questioning his authority.

Later that evening, he called the executive chief and threatened to fire him if he continued to allow me to survey the area. When the executive chief gave his support to the survey, the commissioner installed his nephew as the new chief. It was a big problem. The community refused to recognize their new chief and demanded their chief be reinstated. Chiefs in South Sudan are the only leaders who are elected after every 4 years by their people through a democratic process. The community in Atiaba was very upset and ready to die defending their constitutional right.

I was in Yirol at one of the project activities we were running when I received an urgent message that I leave the town immediately using any available plane at the airport that day. I went and was evacuated to Juba. The commissioner had sent a letter to the CRS country representative, asking him to pull me out of Lakes State because I was getting involved in local politics and turning the local youths against him. Indeed, on the day of my evacuation from Yirol, the commissioner himself came with soldiers to ambush me on the way to Rumbek. He stopped my car on its way and searched it. He was looking for me. He asked the driver, who told him that I had left for Juba. I ended up staying in Juba for 3 months while the situation continued to get worse day by day as youths continued to be adamant in their position of not allowing the new chief to be installed.

The commissioner was mobilizing soldiers to go to the area and fight the youths. It was a worrying situation. One day, I called the governor and threatened to sue him in a court of law on behalf of the community if he allowed his commissioner to send forces to Atiaba to massacre people. He was scared by this statement and asked me for ways to reduce the tension. I told him to reinstate the duly elected chief and allow me to continue my work in Rumbek. The governor agreed. Meanwhile, the situation was still worrying. Some people were trying to exploit the situation by rallying the youths to go and attack the commissioner in his office. Once the commissioner made a public announcement that the chief was reinstated and I was allowed to return, the violence was subdued.

I continued to perform my duties in Rumbek without interference from anyone. However, in November 2018, our project ended, and I had to move to Juba, where my family was to find a new job. I was applying for a job almost every day, but I wasn't being successful. In September 2020, though, I got a job with Water for South Sudan

(WFSS) as its Juba Coordinator. The WFSS was founded in 2003 in the U.S. by one of the Lost Boys, Salva Dut, to provide clean drinking water to the people in South Sudan as well as education on hygiene and sanitation. I was managing the Juba office and coordinating WFSS activities in Juba. I was meeting with the stakeholders and facilitating the movement of cargo being shipped through Juba to Wau in Western Behr El Ghazal State.

I found this to be a rewarding job as I was getting known due to the networking I was required to do with other INGOs. I was also writing proposals, though none of them was funded while I was still at the WFSS. It was a great job, and I was happy that I was part of the organization that drills wells in the villages so people would have clean drinking water and education on better hygiene and sanitation practices. I worked for this organization for just one year and then left.

Soon, a colleague of mine whom I used to work with at CRS gave me a surprise phone call. His call was for me to send him my resume. There was a need for a consultant to help Bor Vocational Training Center (Bor VTC) in Bor, Jonglei State. The Bor VTC was going through a difficult time as its director and his subordinate were not working together as a team. The centre was being politicized, and donors were not happy with the situation and were ready to call it quits. The centre was being supported by Norwegian Refugee Council (NRC) and the United Nations Development Organization (UNIDO) with support from the United Nations Development Program (UNDP). I was excited and happily sent my resume. In the next few days, I successfully passed my interview and was quickly dispatched to Bor to undertake my assignment. I arrived in Bor and found the town submerged under the water. I was so upset by these dire circumstances, but I had to focus on my assignment. Thank God the centre was not affected by the flooding. I was staying in town and had to commute daily to work using a boat in the flooded streets.

Embarking on my work, I had to reconcile the two parties in conflict first before anything else. I told them that I was from Lakes

State and did not have any interest in whatever had created a conflict between the two of them. I added that my only interest was the survival of the centre, and I would do anything to ensure that the team worked together for the interest of the community we were serving. They listened to me, and we discussed their issues. I realized the administrator was doing double work and was just being paid his teaching salary, which made him upset. He also wanted to be paid too for his administrative work. He was the one compiling the reports and in charge of the facility management, including staff. The director, on the other hand, was challenged by the English language and had difficulties in drafting reports. The administrator refused to compile the reports and weekly updates required by the donors. This was jeopardizing funding for the centre. Thus, the UNIDO and the Ministry of Labor, Directorate of Vocational Training, wanted a solution to the problem before the gate of the centre was shut. So, I quickly advised the way forward by making the director agree to pay the administrator for his additional work as a teacher and administrative staff. I also told them that I would oversee the compilation of all the reports, including weekly updates and share them with the donor. After two weeks, things were quickly turned around, and the management at Bor VTC had improved greatly. The UNDP coordinator visited the centre and was impressed with the improvement in everything. He wrote a beautiful report detailing great improvement at the centre and gave me credit for all the improvement.

The centre is now running smoothly, training students for jobs in tailoring, masonry, carpentry, electricity, motorcycle repairs, solar installation, plumbing, hairdressing, and business management. All the students who attended vocational training while I was at Bor VTC started their own businesses upon graduation and made a living.

With improvement at the Bor VTC, I now had another opportunity to rejoin CRS after three years as a field area coordinator in Mingkaman, Awerial County, Lakes State. I would oversee operations, coordination, and security. Awerial County hosts thousands of Internally Displaced Persons (IDPs) who were forced out of their homes in Jonglei State by the 2013 civil war between the Sudan People's Liberation Movement in Opposition (SPLA/M-IO) and South Sudan's government. Over 400,000 people lost their lives because of the conflict. CRS is implementing general food distributions for displaced people, host communities, and flood-affected people on behalf of the World Food Program. It also runs a school meal program.

Youths from the local community were not happy with the way things were being run at CRS and had protested at the gate several times before my arrival. They were threatening to burn down the CRS compound and beat and chase away staff. Internally, staff were mistrusting each other and having grudges among themselves, which ended in violence. For this reason, CRS wanted someone to rescue the situation quickly, and I was the best choice because of my experience in conflict management and my previous experience working with the youths from the local community there. I was hired and rushed to the area to turn things around. I successfully did that within a few weeks, and the community came back to slowly trust CRS once again. I also made sure that some youths from the local community were given opportunities for employment. This also improved the relationship between the local people and the agency.

Working in South Sudan as a humanitarian worker, I came to realize that my decision to cancel the immigration process for my family to join me in the U.S. was the best decision ever because of what I was doing to save the lives of thousands of ordinary people in my home country. Despite many challenges along the way, I feel proud of what I was able to accomplish.

The Scattered Family

A parent naturally wants to be with his family, watching his kids grow. However, this was something that I had to sacrifice for my work. For years since my return to South Sudan, I have been far away from my family – doing charitable work in remote parts of the country. Because of the lack of security and medical services in these areas, I keep my family in Juba, often spending 3-4 months at a time away from my children. My kids always struggle to understand this, and it's increasingly difficult to answer questions like, "When are you coming home, daddy?" or "Why don't you ever come home, daddy?"

I am the father of 4 beautiful young kids, 2 boys and 2 girls. Their ages range between 4 months to 8 years old. I also have a grown daughter who is living in Australia. She is 21 years old. She was born in the refugee camp, but because she was resettled on a distant continent with her mother, I never had the chance to see my daughter. I bear a lot of guilt for not being a father to my oldest child Toto. I can't imagine how painful it was for her to grow up without a father.

My wife struggles every day to accomplish simple tasks because I am not around. She stays home with the kids alone on the outskirts of Juba, but my kids go to school in the city. Like most of the schools across the country, their school does not have a school bus, so they depend on being driven to school every day. If their mother is too busy with the baby, she may not be able to get them to school. I have been contemplating quitting my humanitarian work and looking for a government job in Juba to be with my family, but it has been difficult to find a position. Often, I consider applying to take them to the U.S., where I could offer them a better life, but I fear that would take me away from the important work I am doing for my country.

These days, many South Sudanese families are scattered like mine, with fathers working in the West and South Sudan while their families live in East Africa. I worry about the impact this has on the children who grow up in the absence of their father. I was torn from my family by war. It seems terribly ironic that the work I do now for peace is also tearing me away from my family.

My journey of decades ago has taken me a long way from my homeland, but I have gradually found my way back. In the Dinka language, there is a saying: "A man goes down an unknown path but returns on a known road." I made my home in another part of the world for more than a decade, was educated there and have lifelong friendships there, but my journey has returned me to this road that I have known since my boyhood. This is the place I will raise my children with Dinka traditions and an abiding love for South Sudan.